And They Danced 'Til Midnight

I hope you enjoy my book.

God Bless!

D. William

Illustrations by Shane Church

Come Away With Me
Words and Music by Norah Jones
© 2002 EMI BLACKWOOD MUSIC INC. and MUTHAJONES
MUSIC LLC
All Rights Controlled and Administered by EMI BLACKWOOD
MUSIC INC.
All Rights Reserved International Copyright Secured Used by Permission

And They Danced 'Til Midnight

D. Wilburn

2007

And They Danced 'Til Midnight

TABLE OF CONTENTS

ACKNOWLEDGEMENTS

I would like to acknowledge my mom and my son for being a major part of my life while writing this book. My mom is the motivation behind one of the stories in this book.

I would like to thank Shane Church (trueroots1976@hotmail.com) for his illustration of my stories and the help and contributions he made toward this book.

I would like to thank Barbara Rose for being by my side during our book club days, reading my stories with honesty and enthusiasm, and for her contribution to this book.

I would like to thank Elliot Bader (Ebnli@aol.com) with NLI, inc. for his editing and advice.

I would like to thank the rest of my family, friends, and church for providing much needed support and inspiration.

Inquiries can be directed to Andtheydancedtilmidnight@yahoo.com

For my son and my mom, family and special friends

PREFACE

The ideas for some of the stories in this book just flowed like water. Others were a little more difficult. "I Want To Live" was the hardest to write of all the stories. It reminded of me of when I became pregnant in college and the hard decision I had to make. I would often cry while writing this story. However, my favorite story is "Chicken Feet Stew". This story was from my mother's childhood. She would regal me with many stories of her childhood and this one was most entertaining. I along with my siblings and cousins, too, were a second generation of Ain't Sally's guardianship. I don't quite remember being that mischievous, but we had plenty fun over to her house. I remember the big five cent cookies at the corner store most of all.

"I Have Seen the Mountaintop" is my take on Martin Luther King's speech. I believe each of us has a journey, whether it is fighting for civil rights or just surviving a hardship.

"I Murdered a Snowman" is my ode to Barbara Rose. She loves snowmen and drives me crazy with them around Christmas time every year. I thought she would like the story. She didn't think it was very funny.

"Don't Take Your Gun Today" and "Tell Him You Love Him" were stories I carried around in my mind for many years and finally put down on paper.

"Clothes Make the Man" is an ode to the fashion icons of my lifetime.

"The Book of Kings" is my take on some of the sensational stories I have read in the bible.

"A Mother's Love" and "The Step Dad" are my take on paternal and maternal relationships with children. "Hail" is a story of people who find love wherever they can. I believe anyone who finds love is one of the luckiest people on earth no matter what their age, their sex, or sexual orientation. They're very lucky to me. "Partners", on the other hand, is for people who don't appreciate what they have in a love relationship. Love is too precious to just give away. "Mrs. Peterson and the Preacher" is my take on the lonely and the choices they make. "Big Robert" is a mixture of finding the right person and gaining respect for oneself.

"Come Away with Me", "Hair", "Letting Go", and "Vampire Love" are stories of the choices we make in life and the consequences for our actions.

"Son of Sun" is my take on Global warming. "The Path to Odyssey" is about the political ramification of immigration. What are we letting in or what are we throwing out? Could it be someone who has brought an eradicating illness to our country or someone who can save us from debilitating illnesses like cancer or Aids?

"To Find God in Me" is a startup story of my relationship

with God. It is only my first story about God. I would like to write deeper more meaningful stories on this subject in the future.

The End

CHICKEN FEET STEW

I should have known. My name is Rodger and I'm a chicken and I should have known. I should have known by their smiling faces and their hungry eyes, especially when that big fat one sat in the back yard and ate red sand for an hour. I should have known.

This is a story of eight little bastards, I mean, eight little darlings who lived next door to me. My owner's family and I moved into the neighborhood a month ago. It was a small house with a nice back yard for me. I loved to play in it. I loved to run under the house, jump on the porch, and jump on the fence and just play. My owner was David. He was the only child of parents who were trying to provide a better future for him. Their ambitions took them to many places and that's how we landed here next to *them*.

The *them* I'm talking about are the eight little bas-, darlings who lived next door. Most of them were the offspring of a beautiful black woman who could have easily passed for white. She had coal black hair and dark irises surrounded by a light blue ring. She even had pink nipples. I just happened to catch a glimpse of her dressing one night as I was sitting on our fence with my neck stretched to the max. Her name was Diane. She was on the chubby side, but still beautiful, which often brought her attention from men, whom she had a weakness for, and which often produced a pregnancy. In all, Diane had eight children by at least five different men. Yes, she could have easily passed for a white woman, but she was followed by eight children whose skin colors ranged from black-brown to red-yellow to one as light as her.

Their names, mostly nicknames, were Lucy, Lucky, Little Joe, Sony, Carla, Topper, John-John, and Jason. Lucy and Lucky were grown and lived somewhere else. Jason had not been born at this time. The three remaining little darlings were their cousins, Christy, Turtle, and Punky. They were Diane's nieces and nephew. Christy's mama was in jail for stealing. Her mama would become a master booster and marry a famous gangsta with a city name. Turtle and Punky's mama was dead. A jealous friend killed her in a juke joint one night.

Diane took care of all of them by herself. She mostly had help from her Aunt Sally. Ain't Sally, as they called her, was once married to a bigwig in the A.M.E. church, but as her husband passed away so did her status, and now she was stuck taking care of the kids of a promiscuous niece. She had little patience with them and often took out her Christian hostility on them. Nobody had money, so Ain't Sally would go up to the corner store and by a pound of chicken feet, and then she would make chicken feet stew. Each child would get a bowl of stew with one chicken foot. No one had the audacity to ask for more, because there wasn't any, and if they did they'd get slapped across the face.

So you see they were hungry little darlings. Their meals mostly consisted of red beans and hot water corn bread, cereal with water, and sugar sandwiches. Sometimes Diane would take them to the garbage dump and they would dig for food in the trash. They would often find dented canned goods and raw vegetables thrown out from the grocery store but still good enough to eat. It was survival for Diane. She often thanked God for any grace and tender mercy that was bestowed upon her and her children—and she always thanked God for beans.

Let's talk about the eight little darlings for a while. Their ages ranged from five to eleven. There was Little Joe, the oldest of the bunch, who was as sly as a fox. There was Sony, the oldest girl, who was big and fat for her age. She often had the most responsibility of the bunch. Christy and Turtle were the two adventurers of the brew. Carla was the tattletale of the bunch. She would often get everyone punished with a whooping. Topper, John-John, and Punky were the youngest. They all slept in one room together, and when they spent the night at Ain't Sally's, they all slept on the porch.

Diane worked full time downtown at Titches, a department store. She worked in the cafeteria. Some Black people couldn't work in those positions back in the 40's and 50's. The people at Titches couldn't tell if she was white or black, so they hired her. That meant that Ain't Sally kept the children for her while she worked, but when Ain't Sally had errands to run, she would leave the little bas-, little darlings with her sister, Ain't Louise.

Ain't Louise was totally blind and when she kept the children she would literally tap her cane all day looking for them throughout the house. Of course, the little darlings took advantage of this. They would hide under the bed or in the closet or wherever they could to aggravate her. Their favorite spot was the attic. They would drop rocks, food, or whatever they could find on Ain't Louise's head. Their very favorite droppings were Doodie bugs. Doodie bugs are little bugs that have an oval shape and when you pick them up they roll up into a ball. They would drop the bugs on Ain't Louise's head as she passed by looking for them. She couldn't feel them until they unraveled and started crawling on her scalp. She would then start flailing her cane and yelling like a banshee, "YOU LITTLE SON-OF-A-BITCHES! YOUR MAMA'S A TRAMP! ALL Y'ALL GOT DIFFERENT DADDIES!" The children would all start crying at this cruel, demeaning statement, and when things settled down, they would drop more Doodie bugs on Ain't Louise's head and the process would start all over again. Ain't Louise's only recourse was catching one of the little darlings off guard and then she would beat the hell out of him or her with her cane.

But enough about their life at Ain't Sally's home, let's talk about their life at their own home. Sometimes when Diane would go for her errands or go to work, she would leave Sony in charge. She would threaten all of them with the right hand of God if they left the yard. Of course, the little adventurers never behaved. The boys would go off and get into mischief in the neighborhood, and the girls would find themselves on the corner gossiping and smoking candy cigarettes. When they estimated Diane's return, they would run home quickly, clean up, and pretend they were at home the entire time. This would have worked except for one thing, Carla.

Carla was not only a tattletale, but she held close to her Mama's apron. She was Diane's favorite daughter and Diane bestowed on her a closeness and coddling to be envied and revered. Carla, in turn, bestowed upon her mother all the business of the impetuous gang's comings and goings, and when they disobeyed, Diane would direct Little Joe to go out and get seven switches for each of them. The children would immediately start crying because they knew what was in store for them.

As much as Little Joe hated whoopings, he loved gathering switches for his siblings and cousins. If you were on his good side, he would get you a flimsy switch that still stung, but it was least likely to leave a welt. Now, if you were on his bad side, he would get a long flexible switch that would hurt like the devil and leave plenty of welts everywhere. Little Joe would line up the switches on the bed from the youngest to the oldest. Diane would start with the youngest, calling them into her room one at a time. As beautiful as she was, she could whoop like a Red Demon in high heels. After each whooping, she would simply pull her jet-black hair back behind her ears and yell "Next!"

Of course, this kept all the children home and attentive for a little while and that's where I came in. The first time they saw me, they stared at me in wonderment. David introduced me as his pet, Rodger.

"You got a chicken for a pet?" asked Little Joe.

"Yes, he's my best friend," said David.

From that moment on, the little darlings stayed close to the house. They watched David closely as he played with me, talked to me, and taught me new tricks.

One day I got out of my yard and managed to jump the fence into their yard. Christy immediately yelled, "Chicken!" and they all came running out and started chasing me around the yard. I thought this was so much fun. I was playing. Playing. Playing. I loved to play and just when Punky caught me in his arms, David came outside.

"Hey, gimme my chicken," David demanded.

They all stood still with quarter-sized eyes staring at David.

"Gimme my chicken," David said again.

I heard Sony whisper, "Give it to him." Punky slowly walked to the fence. I know it now, but I didn't know it then. At the time, I could have sworn Punky licked the back of my head as he handed me to David.

One Saturday, as David's family went to visit their family out of town, the little darlings were sitting around bored. I wanted to play. David was gone and I wanted to play, so I jumped the fence and went next door to the children. They were all inside, so I let out a loud squawk. No one heard me, so I let out another loud squawk. The little darlings on the inside couldn't believe what they were hearing. Suddenly Christy stuck her head out the back door, saw me, and yelled, "Chicken!" They all came running out to play with me. I was so glad. I ran this way and that way and they chased me. I was so happy, and then someone yelled out, "I want the wing!" Another said, "I want the thigh!" I instantly realized that they didn't want to play with me, they wanted to eat me. I desperately ran toward the fence to jump back into my yard when someone threw a brick at me and knocked me down. I got up quickly and started running again. They were blocking me from the fence. I tried to jump over their heads when suddenly Sony grabbed me by the head and started twirling me around. I went Whoa...Whoa...Whoa...Crick.

As I looked down from chicken heaven, I saw my poor body being plucked of all its feathers. John-John, Topper, and Punky dug a hole and buried the feathers so no one would see them. Afterward, everyone ran into the kitchen and watched as Sony cut off my head and chopped me into many pieces. Everyone was claiming which part they wanted to eat. Topper said he wanted a thigh. John-John said he wanted a leg. Punky and Sony said they wanted a wing. Out of nowhere came a voice saying, "I want a wing!" Everything froze. They all turned and saw Carla standing with her arms crossed defiantly. "I want a wing or I'll tell." They all looked at her silently, breathing heavily. Sony finally broke the silence and said, "Punky, Carla gets the other wing." And they went back to hungrily and anxiously watching Sony cook me in a big cast-iron skillet.

Somebody yelled, "Make some syrup, make some syrup!" So Sony whipped out another frying pan and put some sugar in it until it started making brown balls. She then added some water and vanilla flavor and everyone got homemade syrup with their meals along with red beans and hot water corn bread. In all, it was the best meal they ever had in their entire lives. It was a deep-rooted satisfaction that they wouldn't encounter again until they all experienced their first taste of love. Like their first sensation of pleasure, they would always remember me as a gift to their empty and incomplete stomachs.

It was late in the evening and the sun was still shining. David had come home and went in the back yard to look for me. He called to me several times, but got no answer. He looked all around the yard. Fear began to grow in his mind and then a soft breeze came from nowhere and grabbed a feather from the hole that John-John, Topper, and Punky had dug. It blew cautiously his way and touched his left shoe. David picked up the feather slowly, then screamed and ran to his mother.

Diane had just come home from work when David's parents marched to her porch. They fervently expressed their disapproval of the actions taken toward their son's pet. Diane defended her children by saying they wouldn't do anything like that. She asked them to come inside.

"Carla!" She called.

Carla came into the room with a calm sedation that you get from being full. "Yes, Mama?"

"Did y'all eat David's chicken?"

"No, Mama," Carla said. She then let out a loud burp.

As they all watched Carla, the realization of what the children had done suddenly hit Diane and David's parents. Diane slowly turned to David's parents.

"Carla never tells a lie. They didn't do it. Now please leave," she said.

David's parents looked at Diane with an infuriated gaze as they slowly left her house. Diane boldly and smugly met their eyes as they passed by. She took a huge deep breath afterward.

David's mother went home and cradled her distraught son. "The little bastards!" She said to herself. Life was too unfair. There were eight of them and one of him. He couldn't fight them all. Such is the life of an only child. They would be moving to a better neighborhood soon. She would go to the pound and pick out a puppy she knew her son would love and cherish, and with time, she hoped and she prayed, David would forget about this cruel ordeal. For now, she cradled her baby and wiped his constantly flowing tears from his face.

Diane went to her children's room and watched them all as they slept. "Lord, I've got some bad kids," she sighed to herself.

They all had smiles on their faces as they dreamed. The last time she saw those expressions was when some white people gave them toys for Christmas a couple of years ago. She wondered what they dreamed. Did they dream about a better tomorrow where chickens ran free in everyone's back yard? She didn't know. She only knew of the reality that would face her tomorrow and a silent wish that they would have left her a thigh.

Yes, I should have known. I watched the little darlings from chicken heaven as they slept and dreamed. They were so content and happy. And as I watched them at that particular moment, I wished I had Ain't Louise's cane.

The End

SON OF SUN

It's our time now. They had warned for many years about the Greenhouse effect, but no one listened until it was too late. Now they avoid the sun. They live in dark places, cold places. But we of the ebony hue can withstand. They tried to wipe us out with a virus, but we overcame. They enslaved us and whipped us. They separated us from loved ones, but now we are the ones who walk the Earth; this Earth, this glorious Earth that they nearly destroyed on every level. We will replant the trees and bring back the animals. We will become great nations again and the kings will once again regain their thrones.

How powerful is your shine that it burns their ivory touch! They try to control from within dark places, but they cannot touch the ground. They do not know the wind or the few drops of rain, but we know the shadows of every corner. Our children can play, run and jump, and their skins are not scorched. They are the leaders of tomorrow and they will know this Earth.

How great are your wrath, your warmth, and your heat. We remember dancing before our God, honoring nature with cherished wisdom and appreciation. Perhaps He will not remember those who abused His trust, His goodness to this Earth. As we journey across new deserts, perhaps in our reverence He will favor us and sprinkle this Earth with heaven's tears to quench the thirst of His dark children, for we are the last and the first. We are the noir descendants of man. We are the sons of Sun.

The End

HAIR

My name is Constance Miller. For the last few weeks, I had been waking up in odd places and I didn't know why. When I woke up, my hair was usually tangled in something in whatever odd place I awoke. Once, I woke up under a bridge surrounded by a bunch of hobos. My hair was tangled in a bunch of bricks. I even woke up in the middle of a city park. My hair was tangled in the bottom of a bush. I could have been raped, mugged, or worse, but I wasn't and managed to find my way back home safely. My boyfriend was very understanding, but even I could see the frustration in his eyes. What was causing these occurrences? Was I under a great deal of stress? Was there some impending doom coming my way?

Was the impending doom the thought of my grandmother dying? She was elderly, but in good health, though I knew she wouldn't live forever. I felt I had reconciled myself with that. No one lived forever. So what was causing these sleepwalking episodes? I searched my brain for answers then realized I had to go. It was time for my hair appointment. I prided myself on my hair. It was straight, course, and strong. People always remarked on how pretty it was. Chantal did my hair. She was a feisty person from the Louisiana bayou. She kept candles, incense, feathers, and weird things around her at all times, but she was good and kept my hair in fabulous condition. Chantal also had a weird brother that I suspected had a crush on me. Whenever he would come around, they would go in the back room and start whispering. Sometimes the whispering would get very heated and

Chantal's brother would then bolt out the back door. He was one weird character.

The only thing that irritated me about Chantal was that she would openly flirt with my boyfriend, Daniel, whenever he would pick me up from her salon. He liked picking me up from the salon and seeing me fresh from the beautician's chair. He always took me out to eat whenever I got my hair done, so it was nice to have him pick me up. I love Daniel with all my heart and wonder if he will ask me to marry him soon. We've been together for two years. Two wonderful years. He is my constant joy. It's just he seems a little distracted lately. It must be my sleepwalking. I wondered what kind of wife I would make if I were sleepwalking all the time? He must be thinking about that too. I had to find the answer to this dilemma, so I decided to see a psychologist.

I chose Doctor Meshie Adamski. He was recommended by the local hospital and offered a reasonable service price wise. He was of medium build and slightly balding. I came into his small office and did the patient thing by lying on his couch. He asked me if I was comfortable.

"Yes I am, Doctor Adamski."

"You know, you don't have to lie down."

"I know, but I'm comfortable."

"What's on your mind, Constance?

"I've been sleepwalking and don't know why."

"Have you done this in the past?"

"No, I haven't. It just started occurring recently."

"No past history of sleepwalking?"

"None whatsoever," I said.

"Are you under a great deal of stress right now?"

"I don't think I am. This sleepwalking has got me pretty stressed out, though."

"Before that, were you under a great deal of stress?" He asked.

"The only thing I worried about was if or when my grand-mother would pass. She's getting up in age, but I am reconciled to the fact that no one lives forever."

"Is that all?"

"I've been wondering if my boyfriend would ask me to marry him. We've been together for two years now, but that shouldn't cause me stress, should it? I mean, it is a big step, but it's a wonderful step."

"That can be very stressful."

"I love Daniel. He brings me happiness."

"Do you make yourself happy?"

"What do you mean?"

"It's a simple question. Do you make yourself happy?"

"I can't remember being happy without Daniel. He's every-thing to me."

"True happiness lies within oneself. If you can't make your-self happy, what are you going to do if you and Daniel should ever break up?"

"That's not going to happen. He loves me."

"Is anything stressful happening with you and Daniel?"

"He's terribly worried about me and it's caused him to be a little distracted."

"I would think it would cause him to be more concerned."

"Oh, he is concerned about me. I guess he's just trying to figure out if I'm wife- worthy."

"Is that what he told you?"

"No. What else could be causing his mood lately?" I in-sisted.

"You tell me, Constance."

"That's got to be it."

"Is it? What are you really thinking, Constance?" he asked.

I couldn't fight the tears. They started rolling down my face. I tried to fight them, but I ended up choking and crying as I spoke.

"I think he is cheating on me and I'm terrified."

"If this relationship should end, what are you going to do, Constance?"

"I don't know. It's everything to me. It's the only happiness I have. I don't know what I'll do if he leaves me. My life sucks."

"I think you should keep seeing me, Constance. I think it's important that you do."

"Why, because I'm so pathetic?"

"You're not pathetic. You're here. You reached out for help and that's what count."

I drove back to my apartment. It was dark and lonely. Daniel had not called. I wanted to call him and ask him to come over and make love to me, but I couldn't. I needed him too much. I think he knew it. I was the lucky one to have him and not the other way around. He was vivacious, articulate, full of life, and totally open. I was a closed coffin. What he saw in me, I will never know. However he did see something, and it brought me to life for the past two years. "Do you make yourself happy?" was what the Doctor asked me. Honestly, I just existed before Daniel.

Just then, the phone rang and it was Daniel. He said he wanted to talk to me about something important. *This was it,* I thought to myself. I said "Okay" and told him I'd wait here in the apartment until he came by. He sounded so strange, so distant. What would I do without him? Life wasn't worth living without Daniel and it was in the back of my mind all along. Suicide. It had crept after me for years, but something would always stop me. Maybe it was my grandmother. She was such a joy to me, but not even her love could suppress the thoughts that clouded my mind for many years. Life was too hard, too demanding, and too painful. I sat in my living room chair for a long time staring at my front door. He would be coming soon and I couldn't see life beyond that point. The doorbell rang.

He couldn't look me in my eyes. We had made love together, laughed together, and even cried together, and now he couldn't look me in my eyes. He said that he needed some time apart from me. He explained that he was changing and needed the time to grow. I sat quietly and listened while my heart was sinking into my stomach. Should I make a scene? Should I scream and holler? I didn't know what to do. I just whispered a small "Okay" and let the love of my life walk out my door, never to return.

I sat there not knowing if I should cry or split my wrist. Time felt as if it had stopped. The phone rang. I let it ring for a long time. It wouldn't stop ringing, so I picked it up. It was my grandmother. She said she felt like I needed her at this moment. I tried to fight the tears. I didn't want to burden my grandmother, but I slid to the floor and broke down.

***

"Has the sleepwalking returned, Constance?" Dr. Adamski asked.

"I haven't had an episode since Daniel left."

"Good. How is the medication working?"

"It's working fine, Doctor."

"Any thoughts of suicide?"

Silence.

"Constance, I can't help you if you don't talk to me."

"I'm better, Doctor. That's what counts."

"You didn't answer the question."

"The medicine keeps me focused. That was the purpose for giving it to me."

"What are you doing for recreational activities? Are you going out? Are you meeting new people? Have you joined a church? What are you doing for enjoyment, Constance?"

"Doctor, I need to be miserable right now."

"But for how long, Constance?"

"Doctor, you have to understand. I was totally consumed by another person. I existed only for that person. I made myself whole within that person and now I'm left with me, and I don't like this person. She's no fun. She's a downer. She's an empty shell. A medicated zombie."

"Constance, you have to find a way to reach into yourself and find contentment. That is the only way someone will see the brightness in your eyes. You're a beautiful person, Constance; you just don't know it yet. I want you to promise me something."

"What, Doctor?"

"I want you to do some form of activity this weekend, even if it is going out to eat. I want you to do something that will bring *you* joy. Will you promise me that, Constance?"

"Yes, Doctor."

"Constance, you have suffered from depression for a long time. With therapy and medication you can find your way to the light."

I mumbled, "Is that a promise?"

"Yes, Constance, that's a promise."

It was the weekend and I actually felt a little giddy about getting out of the apartment. I bathed and put some clothes on and even added some makeup. I was actually going somewhere. It was just to the McDonald's three blocks down, but I was excited. I thought that I'd order a Big Mac with bacon, something good and greasy.

I walked down the first block and men were glancing at me

as I passed by. It felt good. Shop owners were beckoning for me to come into their store and the street vendors were offering up their wares. The attention was wonderful. I finally arrived at McDonald's and there was a line. I stood behind a tall young man and he turned and smiled at me. He told me I looked pretty and asked me my name. He asked me if I lived in the neighborhood. I told him I lived not too far from here. He moved up in line and ordered a chocolate shake and a McChicken. He paid for his meal, got it, and stepped to the side waiting for me. I ordered my Big Mac with bacon, a large order of fries, and a big Diet Coke. Totally super-sized it! I was going all out with my thrill day. The young man smiled at me as I retrieved and paid for my meal—and then I saw them through the window. It was Chantal and Daniel. They were holding each other as they walked from a store to his car. I felt a fury that I had never felt before and ran from the McDonald's toward them. They were both caught off guard.

"IS THIS WHO YOU LEFT ME FOR? THIS BITCH?" I yelled.

"Constance. Oh!" Daniel said surprised. "Chantal, get in the car!"

They both rushed to his car.

"ANSWER ME! I DESERVE AN ANSWER FROM YOU! YOU BASTARD!"

Daniel drove off in a hurry. I threw my Diet Coke at his car and fell to the ground and started crying. Cars were blowing at me to get out of the street, but I didn't care. He left me for Chantal, of all people. It was the ultimate humiliation. A cop came along and lifted me out of the street. I clung to him. I was afraid to let go. I was afraid I'd fall too deep into an abyss and couldn't find my way out. His partner came with their squad car and took me to my home. They asked me if I needed a doctor.

I said no and they left. Despite my trauma, my mind was clear. Damn medication! I didn't want to die now, but I still had tears and they flowed freely.

That night, I woke up in a small crevice next to an abandoned building. My hair was tangled in a leaky water faucet. I untangled my hair and then I saw him. He wore some sort of mask and he was dragging a woman. She was screaming. I hid in the crevice while he threw the woman to the ground. She tried to scoot away, but he grabbed her and then pulled a knife from his coat. He stabbed her several times until she stopped screaming. I was frozen in terror.

I watched as he stabbed at her chest and then took out her heart, put it in a bag, and ran off. I was so horrified that I couldn't move. I laid in the crevice for what seemed like hours, just watching as blood leaked from the woman's body. I finally got up and went to a pay phone and called the police.

They took me to the police station and started questioning me. A Detective Sherman started asking me the traditional questions, and then his questions turned ugly.

"What were you doing out so late at night, Ms. Miller?"

"I walk in my sleep."

"You're a sleepwalker?"

"Yes. I'm under the care of Doctor Meshie Adamski."

"Do you have his telephone number?"

"Yes."

"Where is the weapon, Ms. Miller?" Detective Sherman asked.

"He took it with him."

"Who took it with him?"

"I told you, the man with the mask."

"Yes, you said that. How did you get those cuts on your hand?"

"I was untangling my hair from the water faucet and cut my hand in the process."

"Where's the knife, Ms. Miller?"

"I don't have a knife."

"There's blood on your clothes and shoes."

"I went to see the victim."

"Forensics is going to want to see your clothes and shoes."

"I didn't do this."

"Did you try to help her, Ms. Miller?" Detective Sherman asked.

"I was terrified. I couldn't move. I didn't do this."

"Then you have nothing to worry about."

They poked and prodded me like a lab animal for hours. They finally released me with a warning not to leave town. I went home and crawled into bed. I was so tired, too tired to be frightened or scared. I hadn't taken my medication in days nor had I seen Dr. Adamski. I was slowly sliding down into depression again. I was glad in a way. I wanted to feel sad, hopeless, and full of despair. It's where I belonged. It's where I needed to be.

***

She died on me. My grandmother died. Friends and family gathered around her home and talked about how wonderful she was. I sat in a daze. There's no excuse to hold on is what my mind told me. It told me that constantly. I walked slowly to my apartment and to my surprise Daniel was standing outside. A part of me wanted to run into his arms, but I didn't. I just walked slowly toward the door.

"What are you doing here, Daniel?"

"I'm so sorry, Baby."

"Thank you, Daniel. How's Chantal?"

"I don't want to argue."

"I don't want to argue either. I'm too tired, Daniel."

"Let me make you some coffee."

"I don't-"

"Please, Baby."

"Okay."

We talked for hours. I didn't tell him about the murder or the sleepwalking. I just cried and he held me in his arms. It felt so good. As the night wore on, I grew even more tired. Daniel was kind enough to put me to bed. I wanted him to join me. I wanted to reach out and make love to him, but I just lie in my bed and let him put the covers over me. I slept a very long time. When I awoke, I was surprised to see he was still in the apartment. He made me a big breakfast and ordered me to eat it. I ate heartily. He stood watching me with an odd expression on his face.

"What's the matter, Daniel?"

"Nothing. Are you going to be okay?"

"No, but I'll survive." I said, surprising myself.

"I have to go."

"I know you do. Thank you for last night."

"You're welcome, Constance. I know how much your grand-mother meant to you and I'm glad I could help."

He stood watching me for a long moment and then said, "I'll talk to you later," and walked out the apartment.

That night, I woke up in an isolated lot under a bridge. My hair was tangled in a bolt that protruded from one of the bridge's stone beams. I untangled my hair then hid behind an old car. There was silence and then I heard them. The man with the mask was dragging a woman, but she was fighting him fiercely. She would get away from him for a second, but he would chase after her and drag her back. She fought him like a wild animal trying to hold onto life after being caught in a trap. I admired her from afar. I had no zest for life, but there was something about her struggle that inspired me. She wanted to live so badly and fought hard to survive. I wanted her to survive. I wanted to survive, so I threw a rock at him.

It hit him square in the head and knocked him down, but he still held onto the woman as he fell. I ran to them, yelling for him to let her go. I picked up a big stick and started pounding the man with it. The woman started kicking him until he let go of her. We thought he was unconscious until he pulled his knife and grabbed the woman again. We both screamed. I tried to hit him with the stick, but he stabbed the woman in the heart from behind. She fell to the ground and I stood there in shock. He then turned and stabbed me in the side. I fell to the ground and tried to crawl away until I started losing consciousness. At some point, I could hear the man stab at the woman's chest and remove her heart. At some point, I heard someone yell and scream. At some point, I heard an ambulance siren before I fell into total unconsciousness.

Detective Sherman was at my bedside when I woke up. "Can you speak, Ms. Miller? Do you know where you are?"

"Water. Can I have some water?"

A nurse came and put a cup of water with a straw up to my mouth so that I could sip it. "Go slow" she calmly said.

My head was spinning and I felt nauseated. "Where am I?" I asked.

"You're in County General," The detective responded. "You've been stabbed. It's not a serious wound. You'll recover fine. He cut out her heart like the other one, Ms. Miller. Do you recall that?"

"I don't remember much after he stabbed me. Things are really hazy."

"Ms. Miller, what is your connection to this man?"

"I don't know."

"There are women dying, Ms. Miller. You must know something."

"I don't know." I said starting to moan in pain.

"That's enough," the nurse said.

"She is not to go anywhere. Is that understood?"

"Yes," the nurse answered him.

They were going to arrest me, but then they determined the stab wound was not self-inflicted. Police officers were placed outside my hospital room at all times. Dr. Adamski was called in. He explained my condition to the detectives, but could not offer any clues as to why I was associated with a serial killer. The press got wind of the story and it was total chaos outside my hospital room for days. When it died down a little, I was ushered out the back door of the hospital into a police car and driven home. When a policeman walked me to my apartment, Daniel was there. He looked visibly upset and rushed over to me.

"Baby, are you okay? I tried to see you at the hospital. I couldn't get in."

"What are you doing here, Daniel?"

"Who is this?" the police officer asked.

"This is my ex-boyfriend, Daniel Carne. He's okay," I replied.

"I need to talk to you," Daniel insisted.

"Daniel, I'm tired. I need to get in the bed."

"Baby, please. I need to talk to you."

"Do you want me to escort him out?" The policeman asked.

"It's okay, officer. Come inside, Daniel."

The officer left and we went inside. Daniel started holding me, but I resisted and tried to push away from him.

"Don't," I insisted.

"Please, Baby, I nearly lost you."

"Tell it to Chantal," I said while trying to push him away from me, but he wouldn't let go. I kept resisting but he held on tight and started kissing me. I melted in his arms. I could never resist him. He picked me up, carried me to my bedroom, and gently made love to me for hours. I fell asleep and didn't notice that he had left in the middle of the night. He was going to see Chantal to end it with her.

***

Daniel arrived at Chantal's and entered her apartment. The apartment felt somewhat off center and had a strange smell. He could hear strange noises coming from her bedroom and walked closer to it. He saw Chantal sitting in front of her mirror. There were candles, incense, and a chicken foot with a feather tied around it sitting in front of her. From a large container she pulled out a heart and sat it in front of her. She uttered a weird incantation and pulled out a bag of hair from her drawer. She laid several strands on top of the heart and uttered another incantation then yelled, "Hair! Hair! Constance's hair! Kill her!" and then she stabbed the heart. Daniel ran to her and grabbed her.

"Where is she?" He yelled while grabbing Chantal's arm and twisting it from behind. "Where is she? Tell me or I'll break your arm!"

"You do this to me after what we've been through? Ahhh!"

"Where is she?" He said twisting harder.

"Ahhh! On top of the Nine Building!" She yelled and then Daniel let her go, grabbed the bag of Constance's hair, and ran out.

***

I woke up on gravel with my hair tangled in a pipe on top of a rooftop of a tall building. I wanted to scream, but instead I untangled my hair quickly. And then I saw him. He was wearing that strange mask and watching me. He stood for an eternity watching me. I had to get away, but there was nothing on the rooftop to fight him with. He pulled his knife and came toward me slowly. I had to do something. I wanted to live, not for Daniel, but for myself. For a long time, life had seemed so hard and I just couldn't find joy in it, but seeing how easily it could be snatched away from you, I wanted to just enjoy the simple things like sunshine, rain, and flowers. I had to fight. There was sand and gravel on the ground beside me. As he got closer, I grabbed a handful of it and threw it into his face. While he struggled to clear his eyes, I ran to the exit door and tried to open it, but it wouldn't budge. I turned and saw he was coming toward me. I ran to the side of the rooftop and started screaming, but there was no one around. He came toward me with the knife. I was determined to fight for my life, so I lunged at him and caught him off guard. We both fell backward and started struggling with the knife. I managed to knock his mask off and was stunned to see it was Chantal's brother. He got up and stabbed at my arm but only cut a flesh wound. I got up and ran toward the exit door again and tried to open it. It still wouldn't budge. He came toward me and I tried to run past him. He grabbed me from behind and was about to stab me in my heart when Daniel grabbed his arm and pulled him back. They started fighting and Chantal's brother took a swipe at Daniel with the knife. Daniel evaded the stab and punched Chantal's brother square in the face. He was knocked unconscious and fell to the ground.

After a rough year of trials, Chantal and her brother were convicted. Daniel and I were married. Dr. Adamski said that my progress was going very well. I want to live now more than at any other time in my life. I wish my grandmother were here to see me happy and enjoying life. I love Daniel with all my heart, but I don't need him to make me happy. I have found happiness within myself. My life is worth fighting for and nothing except the will of God will keep me from living it.

The End

DON'T TAKE YOUR GUN TODAY

One, two, three, four, and five times I turn the front door lock to make sure it's secured. One, two, three, four, and five times I flip the front porch light to make sure it stays on. I do things in fives. I guess you could call me a repetitive compulsive person. I guess that's what I am. I have to do things in fives. I don't do everything in fives—just some things like putting my deodorant on five times or checking my mailbox five times; just little things that would drive the average person bananas. I can't say it hasn't affected my love life, but it has. Most guys last about two months, but Steven lasted a whole year. I honestly thought he loved me until I got five messages on my answering machine that sounded like this:

"First message."

"Hey Lisa, we're through."

"Second message."

"Hey Lisa, we're through."

"Third message."

"Hey Lisa, we're through."

"Forth message."

"Hey Lisa, we're through."

"Fifth message."

"And Lisa, just in case you didn't get any of my other messages, we're through." "End of messages."

I thought that was real cute. I really thought it was even cuter when he left his clothes at my house and I cut circles out of the armpits of every shirt and big circles out where his butt goes in his pants. And what a lovely butt he has. Now the whole world will know.

This morning I start my day by taking five sips of orange juice and five spoonfuls of oatmeal. I watered my plants five times. I've learned the hard way to use little amounts of water each time. When I take my shower, I bathe five times. I have to use a mild soap. I brush my teeth and I rinse five times. I go to my scale and I weigh myself five times. When it's time to get dressed, I choose five different outfits before I decide on which one to wear. This time I've decided to wear a blue blouse and black slacks. I thought my blue pumps would be good with this outfit, so I went to my closet, grabbed my shoes, and tried them on five times to make sure they fit. When I was finally dressed, I looked in the mirror five times to make sure I was perfect. It's just an ordeal I have every working day. The weekends are a lot easier, but they still consist of routines of fives.

On this morning, I called the psychic hot line. I do it five times every day and I usually get five different responses ranging from "You'll find your love today" to "Buy that lottery ticket" to "Today is your lucky day." I know it's stupid, but I like it. This time I tried a new psychic hot line. Sheila, my co-worker, told me about it. She swore they were accurate. They predicted she would meet a new guy and now she's engaged. I told her I would try it. I even like the number they give, 1-900-4WE-KNOW. I dialed the number and a woman answered.

"Hello," she said.

"Hi, this is Lisa. I'm a Scor-"

"I know who you are," she interrupted. "Don't take your gun today, Lisa." And she hung up. I stood there looking at the phone. *What did she say?* I thought to myself. Don't take my gun today? What did she mean by that? I called back and another woman answered.

"Hello, this is Carla 179. Who's speaking?"

"Don't you know?" I asked in frustration.

"No, honey, I don't. Give me your name and birthday," she asked.

"The other woman knew my name," I said.

"Would you like to speak to her again? What is her number?"

"She didn't give me a number. She just read my future and said something very weird," I explained feeling uneasy.

"Tell me what she said."

"No, you tell me my future," I insisted.

"Well, you will take a vacation soon and meet a handsome young man who will sweep you off your feet," she said. I hung up.

I began to pace the floor back and forth. Why would the first operator say that? Why would she say something like that on the psychic line? Who was she? How did she know me? I called again.

"Hello, this is Pam 124. Who's speaking?"

"Do you know me?" I asked frightened.

"No, I don't. What's your name?"

"My name is Lisa. Do you know me?" I asked terrified.

"No. What is your sign?"

"Scorpio," I muttered.

"Well, today is your lucky day. Buy as many lottos as you can. You are about-"

"WHAT ABOUT THE GUN?" I shouted.

"What gun? Lady, you're cra-" I hung up. I called back and another person answered.

"Hi, this is Angie 235."

"My name is Lisa. Can you tell me about the gun?" I said slowly.

"What are you talking about? What gun?" Angie 235 said.

"One of your co-workers said I shouldn't take my gun today. Why?" I demanded.

"Ma'am, I don't know what you're talking about. We wouldn't tell you anything like that."

"I'M NOT CRAZY! TELL ME ABOUT THE GUN!" I yelled as Angie hung up.

I started rubbing my temple. This didn't make any sense. I looked at the phone for a long time. I had called four times. One more time and it would be five. I do things in fives, you know. Maybe the fifth call would give me an answer. I dialed again. A voice answered.

"Hello, this is Melanie 098."

"Melanie, can I speak to your supervisor?" I asked.

"Just one second," she replied.

A minute later the supervisor answered, "Hello, this is Page Lee, daytime supervisor."

"Ms. Lee, one of your psychics told me that I shouldn't take my gun today. Can you explain to me what she's talking about?" I asked.

"I'm sorry, you're mistaken. No one here would tell a client anything like that. We're here strictly for entertainment only."

"Ms. Lee, I know what she said. She clearly said 'Don't take your gun today.' Now I need to know what to do, Ms. Lee," I stressed the point to her.

"Miss, I'm sorry, but you are mistaken. Perhaps you dialed the wrong number," she said.

"I DIDN'T DIAL THE WRONG NUMBER! WHAT DID SHE MEAN ABOUT-" She hung up.

I wanted to call her back, but that would mean six times and six was such an ugly number. My mom died on the sixth and my cousin was killed on the sixth. Jeff left me on the sixth. Everything bad happens with the number six. I stood there. There were tears in my eyes. I took a couple of deep breaths and that made me feel better. I started thinking it was ridiculous. This was all ridiculous. I laughed a little to relieve some of the tension. Then I went into my room and sat on the bed. *It was for entertainment,* I thought to myself. I may have dialed the wrong number after all. I looked at the clock. I was going to be late to work, so I checked myself in the mirror five times again. I reached for my purse and remembered the .45 pistol in my drawer.

"What would it hurt to take it?" I said aloud. "I mean, no one knows the future. I'll keep it on safety in my purse." I grabbed the .45 and put it in my purse then left for work.

I was terribly late and my boss was going to chew me out. I was just glad he had some understanding of my condition; otherwise, I would have been fired by now. The parking lot was full. There was no place to park. I had to go all the way to the end of the lot to find a space. *I am so late,* I thought to myself. *Now I have to walk a good distance to the building, which is going to make me even later.*

As I started walking toward the building, suddenly someone grabbed me from behind. I started screaming while he lifted me off the ground and slammed me into the back of the trunk of his car. I hit my head on the trunk bottom and felt a little dizzy. I regained consciousness and started screaming and beating on the trunk door. He started blasting this loud rock music with the bass turned up high into the trunk. I covered my ears. It was so loud. No one could hear me screaming and I could feel the car take off. It seemed to be going at least a hundred. Where was he taking me? What was he going to do to me? I knew what he would do and I was terrified. It was so dark in the trunk that it felt like a tomb. I tried to feel for the trunk latch, but I had nothing to dislodge it with. I felt around the trunk for a screwdriver or something, but there was nothing. He was going so fast and the music was so loud. I stopped fidgeting and took a couple of deep breaths. *Think, think,* I said to myself. *My purse! My gun!* I remembered the gun. Is it in this trunk?

"Oh please, God. Let it be here," I said crying while I felt around the trunk again slowly. "Please God!"

My hands felt carpet all around until I reached over to the side into the crevice where the jack goes and felt something. It was my purse. Oh God, it was my purse. I opened it feeling relieved. The gun was there. There were five bullets in the chamber. I took the safety off. All I have to do is aim. Just aim and shoot the bastard.

It seemed like he was speeding even faster. He hit a huge bump and the gun flew from my hand. I searched for it quickly and found it again. The music was turned up even louder.

I grabbed my ears because it was so deafening. Boom! Boom! Boom! The bass was vibrating my heart. Then the car seemed to sway or turn and come to a complete stop. I got the gun ready. I was going to kill him before he killed me. I had to. I had to. The music was blasting so loudly. He turned it off, but I could still hear the music ringing in my ears. *Oh my God! This is it,* I thought to myself. He was opening the trunk. Sunlight shone in and I couldn't really see him, but I leaped up and fired five times. POW! POW! POW! POW! POW! There was ringing in my ears from the shooting, but I could hear someone laughing in the distance. Through the haze of smoke I saw a police officer holding a strange-looking man in handcuffs who was laughing hysterically. I could barely hear what the officer was shouting into the receiver on his shoulder.

"OFF DOW!" He shouted unclearly.

"OFFICER DOWN!" He shouted again into his receiver.

I looked down and realized I had shot the other police-man five times. Blood was spewing from his chest. He started coughing up blood and it drooled down the side of his mouth. The strange man in handcuffs started laughing even louder. I looked at the blood spreading quickly across the concrete. I screamed. I screamed. I screamed. I screamed. I screamed and I never stopped.

The End

LETTING GO

Gary Carpenter had sat by her bed many times, just watching her die. He couldn't let go no matter what. God had sent him someone to love and he could never let go of that. He brought out the Statue of Lodoc and called to the gods of life and begged them to send Carol back. They would oblige every time.

It began on a trip to the Mayan world of Guatemala. He wanted to show Carol happiness before she left him. Secretly, he was hoping that one of the ancient remedies of the Mayan would save his beloved. She had been dying for months now and all he could do was sit back and watch. He was helpless and hopeless. She was his world. Was it terrible to love someone so much? He felt guilty about bringing her back so many times, but the joy in his heart when he saw her again would overwhelm any guilt feelings. He needed her. He longed for her. He loved her more than God himself and always feared His repercussions, but until that time he would bring her back.

Silvio was a man with a straw hat and he could get you anything. Anything. He particularly preyed on the spoiled Americans who came down to his country eager to spend their riches off of the hard-worked backs of immigrants much like him. Silvio looked at the man with the ailing wife. He saw the deep sadness in the man's eyes. He saw the man's desperation and only thought *Easy mark.* Just how much he would score depended on the man's willingness to believe.

Carol cherished the stars most of all. She looked up to the heavens and wondered if it would be the last time she would see them. She was ready to go. The cancer had taken its toll on her and she was drained. She suspected the only reason she had lived this long was because of Gary. She knew he needed her. *Too much,* she thought to herself. She needed to let go of his love and his desire for her. This life held little desire for her. The cancer ate away her body inch by inch. *I will will myself another day for him and then he must let go,* she prayed. *He must let go.*

Silvio walked up to the man and smiled his brightest smile. *Easy mark,* He thought to himself.

"Good afternoon, Sir. Are you enjoying Guatemala? We have many sites for you to see," Silvio said.

"Yes, I am. Thank you," Gary replied.

"Have you been to the mountains? There are many ancient temples up there. There are temples that hold the key to the mysteries of life: magical temples."

"Magical?" Gary said lighting up like a Christmas tree.

"Yes, sir, magical. Come with me and I will take you on a journey through the hills. We can take paths to pure pleasure, if that's what you desire? Or something more complicated, perhaps. What is your aspiration? Tell me. Silvio can perform wonders. I promise."

"My wife is ill. She has inoperable cancer. Can she be saved? I mean is there something that can be done?"

"Get a piece of your wife's hair and garment and take a trip with me. Perhaps we can find an answer for you. I will meet you here in the morning at six o'clock sharp."

"I will be here and thank you. Thank you very much."

Silvio watched the man as he rushed back to his hotel. "Easy mark. Easy," he smiled.

He left Carol asleep in the room and quietly crept out. The garment and the hair were easy to get. *Hope was springing its head around the corner,* he thought. *A cure, perhaps they will have a cure.* He would do anything for her. He met Silvio at 6 a.m. as expected. He had two donkeys that were packed with food, water, and guns. Gary was curious about the guns.

"All things great and small are on the mountains. Come, we must hurry before the heat comes."

They climbed over the mountains through deep foliage and wide streams. The way grew thicker as they went higher and the humidity was stifling. They stopped by a brook and let the water cool them down.

"It is over that hill. You will find what you want there."

They traveled over the hill and although things were hot and humid on the side of the mountain they had just climbed, the other side was cool and calm. It was a different world. The few people they saw walked in a trance-like state and did not look up at them as they passed by. Silvio took him to a thick-forested area that was darker than the rest of the hill. An eerie sensation started creeping up Gary's spine the deeper they went into this area. *"Turn around. Turn around."* a voice was saying to him, but he was determined. He had to find help for Carol.

They came to a cave surrounded by thick leaves and plants and entered it. The cave had a smell that Gary had never smelled before. It was a mixture of exotic plants, sweat, and cooked meat all at once. They went deeper and saw a small brown man with a face adorned with white paint and jewelry pierced to it. He was ancient, but you could not tell by his actions. He beckoned them closer. Silvio spoke to him in an old language and then he motioned for Gary to give him the hair and garment. Gary obliged and the small man took the items and smelled them.

"It is too late for your wife. Go in peace," the small man said.

"Please, help me. Please."

"Help you?" The small man said and he shot a quick glance at Silvio. Silvio gave a slow nod toward the small man. "How much did you bring?"

"I brought three thousand dollars. Is that enough? Can you help me?"

"Yes," the small man said and he went to the back of the cave and retrieved a statue wrapped in a banana leaf. "This is the Statue of Lodoc. It will bring back whatever your heart desires, but there is a price."

"You can have all of the three thousand. It's yours, take it." He put the three thousand in his hand and grabbed the statue.

"The price?"

"I will pay any price. Silvio, take me to my hotel."

Silvio took Gary back to his hotel quickly. Gary left him and entered the hotel with a new zest for life. *Easy mark*, Silvio thought to himself again and patted the fifteen hundred dollars in his wallet he had just earned.

And that's how it started. Each time she died, Gary would pray to the Statue of Lodoc and the gods of life would bring her back, except they brought her back with the same cancer and she would die again and again.

Gary sat silently by her bedside. He listened to her shallow breathing. He thought about the next time he would revive her. *Another trip*, he thought, *maybe to Australia? I've always wanted to see Australia. You will love it, Carol.* Just then Carol started choking. She was trying to say something.

"Let go. Let go, Gary," She said through strained breath and then she lay there silently.

Gary got up and retrieved the Statue of Lodoc and set it on top of the dresser. He kneeled in a prayerful position on the floor.

"Oh gods of life, bring back my beloved to me. I am nothing without her. I need her smile, her touch, her warmth. She gives me life. Bring back my love-"

He didn't see her, but Carol had gathered what strength she had and forced herself out of bed and went to the dresser and knocked the Statue of Lodoc to the ground. It shattered into a thousand pieces and then she fell dead to the ground.

"NOOOOOO! NOOOOOO!" Gary yelled as he grabbed Carol in his arms. "Why did you do it? Why? You're my life. My life," he cried while rocking her in his arms.

Carol then turned to dust in his arms. As if God had watched everything Gary had done, a strong wind blew into the room through the open window and swept Carol away. Gary crouched on his knees and sobbed profusely. Nothing was left of Carol, but then he looked down and saw several strands of her hair left on the floor. Gary carefully picked them up and put them in a locket with a picture of him and Carol. "God does show mercy to fools sometimes," he said to himself out loud and then a soft breeze came in and whispered, "I love you, goodbye." Gary crouched on the floor, holding himself for hours as if he would fall off the side of the mountain if he didn't. He then went to the side of their bed and knelt and prayed.

"Thank you, Father, for giving me Carol. Bless her and take care of her in your loving arms. I ask for your forgiveness and I ask for Carol's forgiveness. Give me the strength to live a life where I will always cherish her memory. Amen."

The End

TELL HIM YOU LOVE HIM

It was a typical morning. The sun was shining through the mini-blinds. I lay cuddled in Thomas' arms. He was so warm and cozy despite the warmth of the morning sun. It was summertime and the mornings became warm quickly, but Thomas' warmth was of a different type. His warmth was more intimate. I could hear him breathing. I could feel the rise and fall of his stomach. His arms circled my shoulders as if he was cradling a very soft teddy bear. He was so tender, so kind, and so giving. I kissed his fuzzy cheek and he stirred immediately. He gave a long sigh and enveloped me in his arms.

"You woke me, you nutty girl," he said.

"Is that good or bad?" I asked.

"It depends," he answered.

"On what?" I asked.

"If you're putting out," he said.

"Oh, you naughty boy!"

"Well?" He insisted.

We made love for the millionth time. I could have made love to him a million more times and still wanted more.

We were dressing on our way to our jobs when Thomas stopped me by the dresser drawer. "I love you, Kasey," he said for the thousandth time. "I know you do," I said. He was getting ready to start. We had had this argument many times, but I wasn't having it this morning. I quickly went into the bathroom. He followed me in anyway.

"Why can't you say it?" He asked angrily.

"Not this morning, Thomas. I have a very big day today," I said.

"Do you love me?"

"Yes, I do," I said.

"Then why don't you say it?"

"I'll say it when I say it. Now leave me alone. I have to go," I said rushing out.

I didn't want to look back and see Thomas' wounded face. I was going to have a big day full of pressure over my presentation to my bosses. I didn't have time to hash this out with him. He knew I loved him. Why wasn't that enough?

I quickly got into my car and drove away. Why did Thomas have to start this morning? Better yet, what was wrong with me that I couldn't tell the most precious person in my life that I loved him? What was keeping me from it? It didn't matter is what I told myself. I showed him daily that I loved him. Why wasn't that enough? I pulled onto the highway. It was an easy commute to my job today. *"Thank goodness,"* I thought to myself. I couldn't handle the stress of the traffic this morning on top of Thomas' demands. It would have been too much.

I pulled into the parking lot. Ricky, the parking attendant, was there to say "hi." He was a nice guy. I got out of my car and started walking to the elevator. I noticed there was a slight pressure in my chest. It felt like heartburn. Maybe it was from the pizza we had last night. Neither Thomas nor I felt like cooking, so we ordered a double supreme pizza from Mr. Jim's Pizza Plaza. It was so good and gooey and full of calories. We treated ourselves, but now I was paying for it. The elevator came and I rushed in with my briefcase. On the third floor the office was already bustling. My employer only hired true professionals in their company. They were bright people full of ambitions and drive and they knew that being on time was one of the key ingredients to getting ahead in the company. The pressure in my chest was getting a little tighter. I knew I needed to take something.

Everyone was saying "Good luck" to me as I quickly passed him or her by. I thanked them as I walked. There were very nice people here on my job. I quickly ran to Mary-Ann, the main secretary of the office.

"Mary-Ann, do you have something for heartburn?" I asked.

"I'm sure I do," she said and quickly produced two Tums from her drawer.

Mary-Ann was proficient as usual. That was why she was at the top of her game. Everyone came to Mary-Ann.

"Are you nervous?" She asked while handing me a glass of water.

"Are you kidding?" I asked.

"Well, take a couple of deep breaths and try to relax. Here. It's a butterscotch lifesaver," she offered. I started to laugh.

"Mary-Ann, you're perfect," I said smiling at her.

"I know," she said. "Now go get 'em, tiger."

I gave her a wink and quickly strolled down the hall to my waiting audience.

They were all waiting for me in the office. Mr. Jacob, my boss, looked at his watch. I was two to three minutes late. Not good. Not good. Mr. Jacob was a stickler for timeliness. "Hello, ladies and gentlemen. In the interest of time, I'll get straight to the presentation," I said. I brought down the screen and slipped the cassette disc into the recorder. It brought up my presentation immediately. They looked at my presentation with complete interest. I was winning everyone over. The pressure in my chest subsided a little bit. I was so glad about that. I didn't want anything to ruin this. I presented the final slide and let out a deep sigh before I looked at everyone's faces. They were beaming.

"Well done, Ms. Wills. Everyone else is excused," said Mr. Jacob.

They all went out smiling their congratulations at me as they left. Mr. Jacob stayed behind to congratulate me personally.

"Ms. Wills, excellent presentation,"

"Will they use my ideas?" I asked.

"It's very likely, very likely," he said.

The pressure in my chest was starting to return. It was growing tighter and tighter. I grabbed my chest and leaned forward.

"Ms. Wills, are you okay? Is there something you need to do?" He asked with concern.

What was he talking about? I thought.

"Is there something you're forgetting to do, Ms. Wills?" He kept prodding.

My chest was exploding. I didn't know what was happening and Mr. Jacob was getting weird on me. I leaned on the table. Mr. Jacob came closer to me.

"Ms. Wills, have you told him you loved him?"

I blanked out.

I woke up in the hospital. I was on a gurney near the wall in the emergency room. I felt a little woozy. My blouse was unbuttoned a little bit. I sat up on the gurney with my head hanging down. An orderly rushed over to me.

"Whoa, Whoa, Ms. Wills, take it easy," he said.

"Where am I?" I asked.

"You're in the hospital. You fainted," he said.

"No. My heart! It was my heart," I said.

"Ms. Wills, I'm going to ask the doctor to talk to you. Please wait here."

The orderly went to an attractive male doctor who was reading a medical chart. They both looked my way. The orderly went the other way as the doctor was walking toward me. I looked at him confused.

"Is something wrong with my heart, doctor?" I asked.

"It's Dr. Joseph," he said. "You just fainted, Ms. Wills."

"It felt like a heart attack. My chest was exploding," I said.

"Ms. Wills, we did an EKG. It showed nothing. We're going to do some additional tests to be sure," he stated while looking at my chart.

"I just want to know what happened."

"Ms. Wills, are you under a great deal of stress?" He asked and leaned in closer to me. "Is there something you're forgetting to do?"

The atmosphere was getting thick. His faced appeared distorted to me and my chest felt as if it were dropping into my stomach. What was happening? He was so close to me.

"Is there something you need to do, Ms. Wills?"

Why wasn't he helping me? Couldn't he see something was wrong with me? I grabbed my heart. It was pounding so loudly.

"Is there something you're forgetting to do, Ms. Wills?" Dr. Joseph asked. "Have you told him you loved him?"

I looked at him in utter horror. What was happening? I jumped off the gurney and ran toward the exit door. The doctor hollered after me.

"Ms. Wills, come back," he yelled. "Come back, Ms. Wills. Wait!"

I ran out of the hospital as quickly as I could. There was a bus at the corner stop. I quickly jumped on it. It was crowded with people. They were all looking at me as if I were crazy. I sat down on the front seat. I needed to settle my nerves. The pounding in my chest had subsided. Maybe all this was my imagination: Mr. Jacob and that doctor. Maybe my chest pain caused me to have hallucinations. I decided to see my own doctor tomorrow. The bus had gone a couple of miles headed toward downtown near my job when the bus driver looked back and asked, "Ma'am, do you have your bus fare?" I realized I didn't have my purse, but my keys were in my pocket. I didn't know what to do. I eyed several passengers who looked the other way. There was a nice, little old lady staring at me though.

"I have bus fare, honey," she said. I walked to her, swaying as the bus rocked.

"I really appreciate this. I've had quite a morning," I said.

"It's okay, dear," she said rumbling through her purse. "I have plenty. Just let me look a little deeper in my purse. I usually don't forget to bring my pocketbook. I'm not forgetful at my age. Are you forgetful, dear? Have you told him you loved him?" She asked.

I looked at her in terror and ran to the front door and started pounding on it, screaming, "Let me out of here! Open the door! OPEN THE DOOR!"

The bus driver yelled, "Lady, you're gonna break the glass!" He quickly stopped and opened the door. I ran off.

My chest was pounding again. I felt so woozy and dizzy. I had walked a couple of blocks. I stopped and was leaning on a storefront's door. I went in to sit down. I needed some water desperately. I looked around. It was some kind of strange shop. There were curtains and stars on the wall and a bell chimed as I came in. There was a table in the middle of the room. A nicely dressed woman came from behind the curtains.

She said, "May I help you?"

"I need some water, please. I don't feel well," I said.

"Of course, please sit down," she said while leaving to go and get me something to drink. She came back with a glass of cold water.

"Here you go. Drink it slowly."

I began to drink slowly. The water helped a little bit. I started to calm myself. I looked around her shop again in wonderment. "What is this place?" I asked.

"I'm a fortune teller," she said.

My heart started pounding again. I grabbed my head and started rubbing my temples. "This day is so weird. It won't stop," I mumbled.

The lady looked at me with concern. "Would you like me to read your fortune?" She said while pulling a deck of cards from her pocket.

"No," I said. The last thing I needed from her was some made up happy ending to this day and my life.

"I think you need it," she chided.

I started to smile. A little entertainment couldn't hurt this unusual day.

I said, "Fine, go ahead."

She smiled back and started dealing the cards. But then she abruptly stopped and started reading the cards back and forth.

"You! Oh! Tell him you love him," she said.

I got out of my seat slowly. I started toward the door in terror. This wasn't funny.

"Tell him you love him before it's too late," she insisted.

I ran out of the shop as fast as I could heading toward my job.

She yelled after me, "Tell him you love him!"

This wasn't funny. It had to be a joke. Thomas had to be playing a cruel joke on me. I got to my job and ran straight past Ricky to the garage. He called after me, asking me if I was okay. I ran straight to my car. I remembered that I left my cell phone in the car. I got in and I called Thomas's job.

"Ed, let me speak to Thomas," I said.

"He's not here, Kasey. He called in sick."

"Are you and Thomas playing a joke on me? It's not funny. It's not funny," I said upset.

"Kasey what are you talking about? What joke? There's no joke. You just need to tell him you love him," he said.

"Stop it! Stop it!" I yelled while throwing the cell phone at the window.

I threw it so hard that I put a crack in my car window. I started to cry.

"Thomas," I said. "Where are you, Thomas?" I asked myself whimpering. I picked up the cell and tried to call Thomas, but there was no response. I had broken the cell phone. I started my car and quickly drove out of the garage. I saw Ricky come out of his port looking after me. I had to get to Thomas. I had to. I knew it now.

I was driving quickly. The traffic was easy. I was near our home when I ran a stop sign. I hit a car. I sat in a daze for about a minute. I got out of the car. I didn't care about the damage. I just cared about getting to Thomas. My chest was pounding. The other driver started screaming at me as I ran away from the scene.

"Hey lady, are you crazy? Where are you going? We just had a wreck! HAVE YOU TOLD HIM YOU LOVED HIM?!" He yelled.

I was running and my heart was pounding so loudly I could hear each thump. There was a twist in my chest. I fell down. It was so painful. I had to get to Thomas. I had to. But I couldn't get up. I began to crawl, but I managed to get on my feet and start running again. I wasn't going to make it. There was another twist in my chest. "Ahhh!" I yelled. I fell to the ground again. The pain in my chest was excruciating. I couldn't get up. I couldn't get up. "Thomas!" I cried. I started to crawl. The house was nearby. It took all my strength to make it to our sidewalk. I couldn't yell. I crawled to our doorstep.

"Thomas?" I called, barely audible. "Thomas."

He couldn't hear me, so I reached out for what seemed like forever for the doorbell. I rang it and collapsed. Thomas came to the door and looked down then grabbed me.

"KASEY, WHAT'S WRONG?! WHAT'S WRONG?!" He yelled.

"I love you," I whispered. "I love you," I said again and I died in his arms.

The End

THE PATH TO ODYSSEY

The crowd was magnificent that day. It was a grey, cloudy day, but it dared not rain because Collin Davison was about to speak. He approached the microphone and the crowd went wild. After two minutes of applause and accolades they settled down and Collin started.

"What is the one thing that led to the beginning of Space Odyssey II? Was it a severe misunderstanding? What led to the confrontation between the Americas and the world? Our borders are severely unprotected. There are enemies crossing over into our continent day by day as we speak. Someone helped them accomplish this. What if our enemy befriended a person with the charismatic capabilities to overthrow their country and have a government totally opposite and opposing to the Umeradan culture and beliefs? It has happened before, but this enemy is more cunning and dangerous than any enemy Umerada has ever encountered before.

We ignore our southern neighbors severely, paying more attention to our European and Asian neighbors, but there is a world beneath our feet that is thriving and growing stronger each day. But who is supporting our longing neighbors? The drug trade solely supports some countries. They have nothing else to rely on. These people rely on the weakest of the Umeradan public to support their country. What if someone comes along and offers them not only another source of income for their country, but a chance to gain more power through weapons of mass destruction? What country would turn down the chance to gain an advantage over another country?"

The crowd burst into resentful applause and shouts.

"Our borders are so unprotected that Hitler could cross over, shave his mustache, and live as an ordinary citizen." Collin went on. "What are we letting into our country? How many excuses will we live with before something is done? How many lives will be taken before something is done? I fear a deadly repercussion for our laziness. The enemy knows this weakness in our system and will take every advantage possible to come into and destroy our country. The advantage is happening now and has happened in the past. The system is too easy to penetrate.

We need to act now. We need a leader who realizes this shortcoming and is willing to do something about it. Sentimentality has no place in the safety of our Umeradan communities. The enemy knows us. They used our weakness to destroy the Twin Towers on 9/11, and they will use our weakness to destroy us again. Something must be done about our borders as soon as possible. A strong leader must realize this mistake. A strong leader must be willing to act now. The path to Odyssey is a slow and ominous approach, like that of a snake to its prey. We have an enemy with the patience and craftiness to destroy our Umeradan way of life. He has a plan. What leader will eventually know this? Our culture must choose wisely for a leader with a wise foreboding ability to see into our future. This leader must be willing to look beyond emotions and take a stand for the people of Umerada today. RIGHT NOW, MY CONCERNED CITIZENS OF UMERADA!"

The crowd burst into joyous applause while the immigrants scurried away to their homes, apartments, and meeting places. They knew that there would be safety in numbers. Two men were standing nearby. They had just listened to the speech. They were in awe and disgusted at the same time. The men, Jacob Thomas and Mike McMahan, were agents of the government.

"Wow, that was some speech," Jacob said while the crowd dispersed around them.

"Yeah, some would take it as a threat to our enemies. Others would take it as a threat to the immigrants crossing into this country, especially the Hontas. I think he did that on purpose. He's playing on both sides of the fence, especially to the fanatics that hold true to the pure Umeradan concept," Mike said.

"I don't like it. I think he's playing with fire. The election's in two days; let's hope the President wins again."

***

In a research facility in another part of the country, three men in lab coats were gathered. One was particularly anxious. His girlfriend had broken up with him and he could not focus. He wasted some dangerous chemicals near a set of vials containing various toxic liquids.

"Take it easy, Jed. What's wrong with you?" Lab man 2 said coming over to him.

"Nothing. She broke up with me. She's my world. I can't live without her. I can't. I CAN'T!" Jed screamed while shakily holding a test tube. Another lab man came over and grabbed the both of them.

"What the hell are you two doing? Don't you know there are cameras on us? Get yourselves together before we all get fired," Lab man 3 said.

"Fired? I don't care about being fired. I want Jenny back. Jenny! Jenny! JENNY!" Jed screamed and started to throw vials on the floor, crashing them and mixing formulas together. Lab man 3 tried to control Jed by holding him while toxic fumes arose from the floor. Lab man 2 swayed and fell to the floor. Lab man 3 felt Jed go limp in his arms and slide to the floor. Lab

55

man 3 staggered to the red emergency button, but slowly lost control and fell to the ground dead.

***

The news of the deadly virus reached the President's office quickly. Some aides and his trusted Chief of Staff, Elijah Moon surrounded him. Moon was the highest Honta in the land and in the world. He was the President's total confidante.

"How bad is it?" asked the President.

"It's bad, and I fear Davison will take advantage of this situation. There are thirty thousand infected already, thirty more will be infected tomorrow," said Moon.

"We need to do something fast. People are saying the Hontas brought this virus from their land and Davison is jumping all over that. I fear a deadly repercussion. Moon, I need your advice."

"Let's put our two trusted choirboys on this for now."

"I'll get a hold of them immediately, Sir," one of the Aides said then left the President's office.

***

In a place across the country, the family-heads sat at the dinner table while the children played in the other room.

"We must not stay here, son. You heard Davison's speech. The climate in this country has changed. There is bitterness brewing and someone will get hurt. A lot of someone's will get hurt," Sary, the grandmother and mother to the Memon family of Hontas, said.

"How can we leave civilization and go back to the old ways, Mama? This is all my children know. The old ways will be hard for them," Amon Memon, the father and husband, replied.

"Would it be better if they were dead? Your mother is right.

We must get out. We have warnings all around us just as the Jews did before the Holocaust. We must not wait too long," Lail, the wife and mother said.

"Do you remember the old ways?" Amon asked.

"I remember, and there is life there. Don't worry about the children. They will adapt. It will be hard at first, but this is our natural way. It will come to them like the smell of earth after the rain," Lail responded.

"Then we must go now," Amon advised.

***

Jacob and Mike had been briefed on the circumstances of the virus. They arrived at the laboratory where it all started. They were dressed in decontamination suits as they entered the premises. The bodies had already been removed and burned. They walked the lonely halls of the facility. All was in order except for a laboratory with broken vials on the floor.

"This is where it started," Mike said.

"But it must have mixed with another substance or there would have been more deaths. Let's keep looking," Jacob advised.

They went farther down the corridors. The stillness of the place chilled their bones as they walked the halls. Everything was in place as if nothing had happened. There were coffee cups on counters, half-eaten donuts, and pictures of loved ones on individual's desks. It was as if death came calling at a moment when everything ordinary was going on in their lives. Everyone expected to come to work and go home to love ones like any other day, except on this day everyone had wished they had had a look in God's Book of Knowledge early that morning before their cereal.

In one spot, there were pieces of glass vials on the floor near a big vent that led to the outside. On a table near the vent was a case of contaminated vials.

"What was happening here?" Jacob asked. "There's something wrong. Why are these vials here? Which body was found here?"

Mike looks at the data file. "A Marianne Facet."

"Why are these vials near this main vent?" Jacob asked.

"What's different about the vials?"

"They're labeled 'Biohazard.' They're supposed to be stored in a special lab."

"Something is wrong. Let's contact Moon as soon as possible," Mike said.

They traveled back to the Capital to meet with Elijah Moon confidentially.

"Marianne Facet recently acquired $100,000 in her bank account. The election is in a couple of days. We have work to do. I'm sending a sample of the virus to an old Cahorna south of Umerada. She can cure anything. If the President knew I was sending you to a witch doctor, he would have my head, but people are dying at an alarming rate and the scientists are not working fast enough. Take the sample and go to Evalu land and find the Cahorna. She may give you a cure immediately. This is strictly confidential. I will deny any involvement," Moon said.

"What about Marianne Facet?" Jacob asked.

"I have my best man seeking the answer immediately. Go now and stay in touch."

***

They traveled with horses through the terrain, over the border and over the mountains. The way grew denser, deeper, and darker. They were looked upon as unwanted strangers and guns were held tight as they went by. As they came to a trail that led to the Cahorna, bushes arose from thickets. They had to chop their way through jungle forest and swamps with stirring gators waiting to pounce. Mosquitoes took big chunks of blood out of their skin.

Up the trail they traveled to a remote area of the land. On top of a hill was a small hut. Inside was a woman ancient in years that invited them in.

"What you bring is man-made," the Cahorna said. "It did not come from the Hontas."

"Can you provide a cure?" Mike asked.

"Maybe. I must smell it."

"It is very deadly and contagious," Jacob warned.

"Much has tried to kill me. I still live. Stand near the deer antlers for protection. I spray goat's powder to protect you."

The Cahorna went to the fire and threw goat's powder and an unknown substance that brought the fire ablaze. She opened the vial and slowly smelled it. She closed the vial, gathered her potions, and prepared an antidote.

"Here is the antidote, but it will do you no good. Don't go back to your land. It is cursed."

"We have to go back. There are people dying," Jacob said.

"Your nation will die. Don't go back." She gave them the potion. "Here. I can only warn you. Go with God."

They exited the hut and were on their way back to Umerada. Mike's cell phone rang and it was Moon. He was frantic.

"Davison has won the election. He blames the virus on the Honta immigrants. They are killing Hontas everywhere and people are dying at an alarming rate. We investigated Marianne Facet. She was paid to release a similar but harmless virus to the public to stir up sympathy against the anti-immigrant cause, but something went wrong. The virus is deadly and-"

"We have the antidote," Mike shouts.

"You must hurry. Davison has decided to build a wall around the country to keep the Hontas out. I'm leaving for-"

They heard guns firing and the cell died.

"We have to hurry back," Mike says.

They rushed back to Umerada. When they got there, a massive wall was being built around the border. Hontas by the thousands were trying to get out of Umerada and trying to get into Umerada before the wall was completed. There was a thick crowd of Hontas stranded at the border like a beehive. They were met with angry protesters and the army.

Over the radio, Davison spoke. His voice blasted over the loudspeakers so that the border crossing Hontas could hear.

"We must defend our nation from the enemies. Look what they have brought to our nation. They have brought DEATH, DEATH, DEATH, AND WE MUST RETURN THE FAVOR!" Davison yelled.

The wall was almost complete and Hontas were scrambling everywhere. The ones trying to get in were crossing the river by the thousands and Mike and Jacob were with them. They started to scream at the soldiers.

"WE HAVE A CURE! WE HAVE A CURE! WE HAVE THE ANTIDOTE! WE HAVE THE ANTIDOTE! WE'RE UMERADAN! WE'RE UMERADAN!"

The soldiers did not hear them. The wall was almost finished and one more block would close off the border. Hontas were trying to scramble in and out at an alarming rate. The Army opened fire, killing many in the crowd. Mike and Jacob were among them. The antidote fell from Mike's hand, rolled down into the river and disappeared. The wall was enclosed. Running Hontas picked up their dead and wounded and returned home.

✳✳✳

Amon was building a shelter for his family. He was deep in thought.

"We left in time," he thought to himself. "My mother was right. She has saved our lives. Beyond those walls is a country of immense wealth and technology. Beyond those walls is death. We must remember the old ways again. Mother will teach us. She will be patient and understanding. My son plays with his computer game. The batteries will run out soon and he will cry. When he cries, I will comfort him and wipe his tears and then I will take him and teach him the 'Reeason' as my father taught me and his father taught him. This game made me laugh many times. It made me strong. I will make my son happy and strong. We will learn the old ways again. We will survive."

The End

HAIL

I
Stephen

My name is Stephen Grey and I am traveling with my lover, David Cohen, in Germany for the summer. We both just graduated from college and this trip was a present from my parents. David graduated with a degree in Psychology and I with a degree in History. I love history, especially everything about World War II. This war was a clear case of good versus evil. There were no underlying causes or secret vendettas for this war. At that time, the world needed us and we simply responded.

David wanted to go to the Bahamas, but it was natural that I chose Germany for our summer vacation, especially since I speak German fluently. We came here to be treasure hunters, so to speak. I decided we would travel the country searching for old artifacts and relics from WWII. The Germans have magnificent minds and during the war they invented many things. America has its space program because of the WWII-era Germans, and I've heard of other discoveries that have made people rich, but it's not wealth I'm looking for. I'm looking for a part of something great that I can have for my own, just a little piece of history that I can store on my shelf and watch and wonder what it was like during the "Great War." I'm just glad David is willing to go along with my antics. He pretends to be annoyed at times, but I know he's a kid in a candy store just like me.

David is my second lover, and while I am blond and blue-eyed, David has dark hair and dark eyes. I am Christian and he is Jewish, but he doesn't practice his faith. My first lover was Kenneth. He was kind, warm, giving, and he made me laugh constantly. He was two years my senior and graduated ahead of me. When he left for Chicago to start his career in Economics, we drifted apart. I was devastated at first—until I met David. He was and is a quiet, gentle person who's always slow to speak. When I first walked up to him, his eyes lit up like a sky full of fireworks. We haven't made love yet, or even kissed, and I'm not pressing the issue. I've often wondered if he's really gay, but my "gaydar" registers off the Richter scale whenever he's near me. I wish I knew if he had suffered some abuse in the past. He shies away from physical contact sometimes. I want to reach out and touch him so bad, but there is something inside me that tells me to wait. I'm willing to wait as long as I can for him because I am deeply and completely in love with him. He utterly takes my breath away.

If my parents were accepting of Kenneth, they were crazy about David. David has a natural way of bringing out the light-heartedness in both of them. I remember when I told them I was gay. They both cried, but eventually they accepted it because they wanted me to be happy. When I have a relationship problem, Dad listens attentively. He tries to understand and offer advice, but it's something usually far-fetched. The truth is I think his advice would be totally obtuse even if I were dating a woman. Mom, on the other hand, listens and comprehends with a perception that is quite startling. She must have been a gay man in another life. She worries about the lack of physicality between David and me, and she urges me to talk about it with him, but I'm willing to wait. David must come to me. I don't know what is in his past, and there are times when he withdraws into a shell. I don't know where he goes during that time, but he always seems grateful that I am near.

Germany is beautiful this time of year. We were in between Berlin and Dresden in a small town called Duale. It was near a thick forest whose trees stretched beyond the horizon. We have taken many walks through the forest and down the country roads. The local townsfolk pass by and wave to us. They have smiles on their faces and few worries. Every now and then we come across a wall or a gathering of stones that must have been there as far back as the Roman rule. I stare at them with complete awe and wonder, *Did Charlemagne stop here?* I often sit pondering, and when I do, David sits and stares at me with compelling interest, wonder, and amusement. He often catches me daydreaming and when I notice him looking my way, he simply laughs and starts running, expecting me to chase after him. I do, hoping that when I finally catch him we will fall down to the ground and make love to each other. We just end up tackling each other, which isn't so bad either.

Today we are going to thrift stores throughout the small towns hoping to find items of past glories. We are in the middle of Duale's downtown and it is a warm and nice day. There are honeysuckles everywhere and sometimes we'll see a hummingbird or two tasting the sweet nectar of honey that comes from the flower. Honeysuckles grew on the side of my house when I was a little boy. I can taste a honeysuckle's nectar and recall the tiniest details of my childhood, like the first Canadian nickel I found underneath a rock. I thought I was the richest kid in the world.

David pointed to a store on a corner. The sign read "Past Thoughts" and it had blue and yellow awnings hanging above its window. We walked into the store and I immediately felt like a kid searching for the perfect toy at Christmastime. David's eyes lit up like a Labor Day parade, but he would never admit his excitement to me. He's still pretending to be disinterested and sore at me for bringing him on this trip. There were so many things to look at: dolls, furniture, jewelry, clothes, and much more. I marveled at it all while David seemed fixated on a little brown book with tattered leather bindings. He went to retrieve it and started reading it. Whatever was in that book, it captivated him and held his interest. I was still consumed with everything in the store when the storekeeper walked up to the counter. I don't know why, but I felt an odd sensation as I walked closer to his counter. He was a little odd man with gray receding hair and when your eyes met his, you saw they were so deep and sad that you fell into his pool of shame, one from which there was no inevitable return. An overwhelming sense of de'ja'vu hit me so hard that the air felt thickened, like a force field trying to keep me from him. I walked toward him very slowly, staring at him for an eternity.

"I know you," I finally said.

In broken English, he said, "No, I don't know. Never left Germany."

I was about to say something when David yelled to me, "Hey, there's a downstairs!"

My mind left the storekeeper and caught sight of David as he was descending the stairs. He still had the little brown book in his hand. I quickly followed him. David stalled at the end of the stairs and slowly stepped into what I figured must be a basement. I landed a few steps behind him when I saw it. I stood next to David in complete awe and we were speechless. In front of us was a gallery of Nazi uniforms, handguns, rifles with bayonets, thigh boots, and much more. I let out a soft chuckle. David must have heard me, because he put his hand on my shoulder and let out a loud laugh. I turned to him, grabbed him and hugged him, and we started jumping up and down like two children. It was the find of a lifetime, at least my lifetime. I left David's side and started looking closely at the treasures. There were uniforms with swastikas on them and I couldn't wait to try one on. One jacket fit like a glove. I started looking for the pants while swinging a bayonet pretending to fight a dragon. I didn't notice David's reaction. He seemed to withdraw into a corner and his eyes were so sad. I looked up at him, and he smiled a faint smile at me. In my total excitement, I had forgotten that David was Jewish.

I walked up to him and said, "I'm sorry, David. This must be tough for you."

David looked down at the little brown book and opened it.

"It's a diary, a diary of a little girl living in one of those camps. She writes, 'I saw a flower in the corner of the ground near the chained gate. I reached for it and held it tightly near my chest. I realized it was a symbol of my God talking to me. It told me that in hesitant times we must find Him in anything of beauty and He will be there. I have kept the flower for many days and hours, especially during the absent moments. They say my day is tomorrow. I will see my God and be cradled in His arms. There will be no hesitance or absence, only light and flowers.'"

David opened the book further and there was a pressed daisy near the back of the book.

"That is beautiful," I said, and for some unknown reason, maybe it was the way David was holding the little daisy or maybe it was the way the stair light hit his face, I reached out and caressed David's face as gently and sensuously as possible. He immediately recoiled.

"Don't," he said and walked away.

I don't know why I got so angry. Maybe it was built up sexual tension or maybe it was because he had not let me into that dark shell yet, or maybe I just needed him 100% and he wasn't there. I don't quite know, but I blew up as David walked away.

"Do you think I'm a machine?"

"Stephen, please."

"Don't 'Stephen please' me! How long do you expect me to wait?"

"I don't expect anything from you."

"How dare you, David."

David started walking away.

"DON'T WALK AWAY FROM ME, DAVID!"

The storekeeper heard us arguing. He started shouting in German, *"I'll call the police! What's going on?"*

I immediately ran upstairs to quiet the storekeeper down. David was left alone. He was falling into that dark place again. I didn't know how much I played a part in keeping him from falling into his pit of hell and suffocating alive. I know the memories were starting to flood back into his mind until he saw something strange underneath a uniform coat. He walked slowly toward it as if compelled by a magnet. It was brown and at least three feet long and four inches wide. It had strange markings and buttons on it. There was one big red button on it and he hesitated to touch it, but finally he did. It started to hum.

After convincing the storekeeper that there was just a small misunderstanding and everything was fine, I quickly walked back down to the basement feeling totally guilty for what just happened between David and me. I needed him so much and I didn't want to lose him. I would wait for him forever if I had to. I had to convince him of that. I walked down into the basement and saw David holding a brown object—and then he disappeared right before my eyes.

II
David

I woke up in a dark place. Where was I? I definitely wasn't

in the thrift store. The floor was cold to the touch. It was dark, so dark. Someone was coming. A door was opening and someone was stepping into the light. He had on a uniform. He came closer and I saw the black swastika on his arm.

"Hail, Hitler," he said slowly as he walked toward me.

The silent screams had returned.

III
Young David

My name is David Cohen and I live in a small predominately white neighborhood. I say predominately because of the pretty black girl who has just moved into our neighborhood. It's a quiet neighborhood where everyone minds his or her own business. Unfortunately, the neighborhood is so reclusive that no one knows each other's names or familial status. They do know a black person has moved into the neighborhood, but they don't know that I am living with my dad, a madman. He beats me and does other things to me that I dare not speak of. He says he will hurt me even more if I scream or cry, so I silently scream and hold my tears until later when he is asleep. My mom died a couple of years ago. The teachers pay no attention to me at school. They know that I am quiet and that I do my work. I dress simply, I'm clean, and I stay to myself. They don't quite know how to take me or they don't want to know anything about me. Whatever it is, they don't get too close to me. Maybe it's a sense of impending doom that keeps them away or maybe they don't care. I don't know. I do know I live a daily hell. There are days when he leaves me alone. I cook his dinner and I try to cook a lot so he will get full and happy. When I do, he usually sleeps through the night, and on those nights I have my tears in peace.

Some days he goes down to the basement and works on his special project. On those days I sometimes sneak outside into my backyard and try to play, and that's how I met my new neighbor, Sophie Middles. She was black, beautiful, and scared. She was receiving calls at night threatening her to move away or else. She had invested all her money into her house and she would lose everything if she moved. She was terrified all the time. When she saw me playing alone, somehow she knew what was going on inside my nightmare. I don't quite know how, but she knew. She would leave me candy bags by the fence some days. I would sneak them into my room and have small pleasures at night. She says she wants to help, but she's scared, terribly scared. Once, I snuck back into the house and Dad was standing there.

"What you say to that Sambo bitch?" He scowled.

"Nothing, Daddy, nothing," I pleaded and it started again.

I wondered many times if the silent screams would ever go away?

IV
Sophie

I saw them. I saw it one night. I wanted to scream and I wanted to call the police, but before I got to the phone, it rang and it started again for me. The voice was always ugly, "Go home, Black Bitch, or I'll fuck up your face." I always hung up as quickly as possible, but this was my private nightmare, my private hell. I didn't know what to do. That real estate agent was so friendly and so willing to accept my offer. I should have known. I was too willing and too happy to buy my first home and now I felt trapped like a small child whose head was stuck in between the railings of her crib. This house wasn't worth losing my life over. I had to leave, but what about David? I had to help him in some way. I just wasn't welcome here, and I didn't know who I could turn to or who would help. I needed to make a move quickly if I was going to save David's life.

The phone calls were getting particularly abusive. I called another real estate company and they offered to help as much as they could. I rented a truck to pack my things and send them to storage. All this was costing me a fortune, but it was going well. I found an organization close by called Child Service National that helped abused children. They were very hesitant at first because they had just been through a brutal lawsuit, which they lost and the child was returned to an allegedly abusive situation. No one was happy when I came inside their organization.

"May I speak to someone?" I asked as I entered.

One of the workers looked me up and down with a sneer as he directed me to the supervisor. The supervisor was sitting behind a tall desk typing. He barely said hello.

I became angry and said; "This is very dangerous for me too. I don't know if the wrong person has seen me come through these doors."

He looked up from his desk then. There was an apology in his eyes as he said, "I'm sorry. Please sit down. My name is Wallace Earlin. Call me Wallace. What can I do for you?"

"I'm afraid for a little boy, David, who lives next door to me. He's being abused by his father," I said reluctantly.

"How do you know this?" He asked cautiously.

For the first time I really looked at Wallace. He was blond and blue-eyed. His looks bordered on beautiful and I wondered what he was doing in a place like this. He should have been on a runway, but David was the issue at hand right now.

"I saw," I whispered, trying not to remember.

"You saw what? Mrs.-"

"Miss Middles. Call me Sophie. I saw," I said as a tear ran down my face.

"Sophie, will you testify?" Wallace asked while coming around the desk and handing me a tissue. I then noticed that he was tall.

"I can't. I'm already in trouble. I've been receiving phone calls. You know the kind that my color receives when they move into the wrong neighborhood."

"Sophie, listen-"

"No, you listen! I don't know who saw me come in here. I'm doing what I can, but I'm, I'm terrified." This time the tears flowed heavily.

Wallace bent down and hugged me softly. For some reason, I grabbed him and let all my emotions out on his shoulders. "I'm sorry," I said while letting go.

"It's okay," he said gently. "Are you moving?"

"Yes, I'm moving today. Please help him. Please!"

"Sophie, without your statement, we can't just barge into this man's house. David has to give us something. Will he turn in his father?"

"I don't think he will and he'll end up dead if something is not done. Please see what you can do. I'm getting as far away from this nightmare as possible. I want to just take David with me-"

"That's kidnapping and a whole set of new problems. Try to get to David as soon as possible and I'll be there with a policeman."

I rushed home. The moving truck was already there and they were packing in a hurry. They said a storm was coming and they wanted to get done as soon as possible. I went inside my house. They were nearly finished with everything. I went to the back yard and looked for David. He was there with a sad look on his face.

"Don't leave me. Please don't leave me," he said quietly and desperately.

"Come here, David," I said moving as close to the fence as I could.

David looked over his shoulder to see if his father was coming. He cautiously moved closer.

"I need you to scream, David, for your life. Scream, David, Scream! Please, baby," I said and gently caressed his cheek.

"Goodbye," I said and rushed into the house.

V
Young David

I heard the truck leave. My friend was gone. The only friend I've had since Mom died and she had left me. I wanted to scream, "Come back," but it wouldn't come out. I wanted to cry, but I couldn't. I would have to wait until tonight to cry and that in itself was worth screaming about. I walked slowly to the house and went inside. I didn't even see Dad standing there.

"What were you and that Black whore talking about?" He said venomously.

"Nothing, Dad, she's just moving," I said sullenly.

I didn't even notice the hostility in his eyes because I was too overcome with grief. He grabbed me by my arm and started yanking me around to face him. I had seen that look too many times. It told me that this time it would be very bad. Someone was knocking on our door. My father looked startled for a second.

"You stay back here," he snarled and walked to the door.

"Who is it?" He said through the keyhole.

"This is the police. Open up."

He opened the door slowly. "What is this about, Officer?" He said politely.

"We're here to investigate allegations of child abuse. Do you have a son named David?"

"Yes, I do. DAVID! DAVID, COME HERE!"

I walked up to them slowly. I looked up at Wallace and the police officer. I thought Wallace was the most beautiful man I had ever seen. I watched the police officer and his gun in awe.

"If you have any questions for my son, ask them now."

Wallace bent down and carefully talked with me. "David, I'm Wallace Earlin with Child Service National and this is Officer Mike Wachic. We investigate child abuse cases. Is there something you want to tell me? We're here to help you. We'll take you to a safe place. Just tell us, David," he said softly.

I thought about what Sophie had said, "Scream, David, Scream!" But I couldn't. I felt trapped like a sheep cornered by a mountain cat.

"Nothing is wrong," I said quietly and grabbed my father's hand.

"Okay, you got your answer. Now leave."

"We will be watching you," Wallace said frustrated.

"GET THE HELL AWAY FROM MY DOOR!"

Wallace wanted to hit him, but the police officer grabbed his arm and pulled him back.

"It's over," the officer said as the door was slammed in their faces.

"We have to do something. He'll kill him," Wallace said.

"We can't do anything. I have to go. Are you coming?"

And they walked slowly to the police car and drove off as my Dad watched through the window. He then rushed up to me in the kitchen.

"YOU TOLD!"

"No Dad, I didn't. I promise I didn't," I said whimpering while backing into the kitchen corner. He drew his hand back to slap me and then he thought of something.

"I think it's time to introduce you to my special project," he said while backing away from me.

"You move and I'll hurt you worse than you've ever been hurt before," he said and headed down to the basement.

I heard him moving back and forth. I knew this would be bad, but my fear wouldn't allow me to move. He was walking back and forth in the basement and I wondered what terror he was preparing for me. He had stopped walking around and slowly started ascending the stairs. I heard something grate on the step as he was climbing. I couldn't run. My legs felt like they weighed two tons and I knew I needed to run away as quickly as possible. This time would be really bad. He emerged from the basement with an evil devilish grin and then I saw it. It was a long black axe embedded with nails, rocks, stones, and sharp metals and he was coming toward me with it. I tried to scream, but only silence was coming out.

"You told our secret to that slut. You're gonna pay. You gonna pay, boy."

I was screaming loudly but nothing would come out, nothing would move. The axe was making a clinking sound as it scraped the floor. The tears came this time. I couldn't hold them. Terror had gripped me and it was choking the life out of me. He was getting closer.....

VI
Stephen

What the hell just happened! Did David just disappear or were my eyes playing tricks on me. I looked around the basement and he was nowhere. What was going on! My mind must have been playing tricks. He must have gone back upstairs. I went back upstairs and the owner was looking at me cautiously.

"Did David come back upstairs?"

He said no and scurried away to the little back room he called his office. I went back downstairs and called for him, but there was no answer. I chuckled to myself a little bit. This was ridiculous. "David!" I called while an eerie feeling was creeping up my spine.

I remembered David was holding something. I saw the brown object on the floor near a stack of uniforms and I walked closer to it. I saw the red button on it.

"What is this?" I said aloud.

Another wave of de'ja'vu hit me and I knew something was very, very wrong. I also knew the storekeeper was part of it. I ran upstairs taking the brown object with me. I immediately went to the back of the store where his office was. He recoiled into a corner when he saw me. I ran to him, dropped the brown object, and threw him up against the wall.

"WHERE IS HE?" I yelled while grabbing his shirt collar and nearly choking him to death. He gasped for air while saying the words, "I don't know! I don't know!" He looked at the brown object and looked back at me.

"You don't, huh!" I said and I threw him to the floor and started dragging him toward the brown object.

"We'll just see what this little thing can do," I said and he started thrashing violently while I was dragging him.

"NOOOOO! NOOOO! PLEASE NOOOOO!" He begged, but I didn't care, I wanted David and I wanted to find him now.

When I grabbed the brown object, this little old man had the strength of five men and he started lashing out at me like a wild animal. I hit him in the jaw to stop him from moving and he lay still for a second. I was about to push the red button when he started thrashing again. I held him down while yelling, "WHERE IS DAVID?"

"PLEASE NOOOO!" He begged with pure terror in his eyes and I pushed the red button.

VII
David

I couldn't scream. Nazis surrounded me and I couldn't scream. They were whispering among themselves. The sinister one had slammed me into a chair and I sat there watching a group of Nazis talk about me as if I were a lab animal.

I gathered the sinister one's name was Michel. He came toward me and said in German, *"What is your name?"* I knew enough from Stephen to know what he was asking.

"My name is David," I replied.

"Ah, you are American?" He said in English.

"Yes."

"David what?"

I couldn't speak. I wanted to cry, but the tears wouldn't come.

"David what?" He said and this time he grabbed my ring finger and broke it.

My body shook with agony and fear.

"COHEN!" I yelled out.

"Ah, American and Jewish," he laughed and the others joined in. He went back to the others and they started whispering again. I grabbed my finger and tried to fix it, but it was searing with pain. One of them came toward me and roughly checked my pockets. They found my wallet. It had my I.D. and credit card in it. They searched through my wallet and a letter from Stephen fell out. The sinister one read aloud in German:

My darling David,
How wonderful it is to have you in my life. When I think of you, joy fills my soul.

Stay with me forever and I will cherish your presence like an oyster cherishes the sea. You are my pearl, a perfect round pearl. Let this pearl's eternal circle remind me of the love I will always have for you.

Always,
Stephen

They all started laughing. Someone yelled out, "A fairy!" Another said, "An American Queen." They all stopped laughing and looked at me with a deadly seriousness. It sent a chill down my spine. They started toward me. The sinister one spoke, "*Nein!* Leave him to me," and they all turned to me and started sniggling. One said "Yah! We will leave him to you, Colonel Archel."

My eyes glistened over. The silent screams were trying to burst from my lips but wouldn't come out. I never practiced my faith. I guess because, with so much pain in my life, I never believed in God. Yet and still, I've even heard of the famous torturers of the Holocaust and I was being left alone with one, Colonel Michel Archel. Michel Archel, forever known as "The Archangel."

VIII
Stephen

I pushed the button again and nothing happened. I pushed it again and again. Nothing. I fell to the side of the storekeeper breathing heavily, letting the brown object fall to the side. He had started whimpering.

"Where does it take you?" I breathed heavily.

"I don't know," he said.

I quickly reached down, grabbed him, and started choking him. "WHERE DOES IT TAKE YOU?" I choked him harder.

"I don't know," he said gasping.

"Perhaps I should try it again," I said and reached for the brown object again.

This time he got out from under me and tried to run. I pushed him toward a stack of dishes and they fell with a clanging, crackling noise. He slipped on one of the broken dishes and blood was oozing from his knee. I grabbed him again and threw him on the floor with the brown object in my hand. I pinned him with my knee.

"Maybe this time it will work," I said and he started thrashing at me again, but now he was weaker. I pressed the brown object to his face.

"Tell me where he is or I'll press the button and this time it'll work."

"I DON'T KNOW. PLEASE PUT IT DOWN. PLEASE!" He begged and I pushed the red button again. This time it started to hum. With the strength of a madman, the storekeeper knocked the brown object over to the corner where a big doll was sitting. An electric current came out of the brown object and the doll disappeared.

I looked at the corner slowly, released the storekeeper, and walked toward where the doll had been. I felt the open air and there was warmth and a smell of electricity. The storekeeper was crying violently. I wanted to cry too. Where was David? Where was my love? If he only knew how much I needed him.

"Please, I'm begging you. Tell me where he is. I beg you. Please tell me."

And a tear ran down my face.

The storekeeper looked at me with a cold blankness on his face and said, "He's in Edilutz, the concentration camp."

The blood ran from my body and I couldn't breathe for several seconds. I whispered David's name, but I couldn't hear myself. I recoiled from the brown object then looked at it again. I whispered David's name again and still couldn't hear myself. With all my German knowledge, I was now faced with the horror of mankind. How easily we can be cruel to each other. My knowledge of World War II had come around to bite me. I knew of the glamour, the richness, and the power of the era, but did I really know of the suffering of the people who had lived through it? Did I know the ones who sat and watched while their country tried to fulfill its destiny through brutality, or the ones who watched as loved ones were taken way to war or to concentration camps, or the ones who watched and just found themselves lost in the turmoil of their times? I was part of their world now.

IX
David

He looked at me with warm eyes. Yes, warm eyes that were almost angelic in appearance, and when they were at their most kind was when he struck with the deadly accuracy of a cobra attacking its prey. He just looked into my eyes as he pummeled each limb. He had crushed all of my fingers before he started on my arms. I couldn't do anything but moan as he did it. The silent screams were back big time. He was about to strike again when one of the Nazi officers came rushing in. He screamed in German, *"A doll, Archel, a doll! Come quick!"* The Archangel immediately left me and went with the officer.

I sat there in pain and thought about Stephen. What must he be going through right now? My father trained me to hide my emotions well and it was causing me greater wrath because of my inability to scream. "I'll hurt you worse if you scream," he would say while he did unspeakable things to me. I sometimes felt as if I had no emotions left. The Archangel was torturing me and I didn't have the ability to scream. He's killing me and I didn't scream. What had my father done?

"A doll! A doll, Archel! Something is coming, I'm afraid. We must hide *The Mead* before something deadly comes to us. We must kill the homo as soon as possible before others come after him. Get Sheep! Tell him to get as many Jews as possible and prepare the gas chambers." Archel immediately agreed, but he was not quite through with me.

X
SHEEP

I knew they would come one day. I just didn't know when. The two Americans. Nobody knew who I was and I have aged very badly. Every once in a while an old soul will come into my store and remember the past. They say, "Sheep. It's Sheep" under their breaths and quickly scurry out of my store. I pulled the lever that sent thousands of Jews to their deaths. I counted them in as they entered the chamber and then I pulled the lever letting in the deadly gas that killed so many. This was my job or this was my salvation. It was the only way I could stay alive in the camps.

He came one afternoon, the dark-haired one. They played with him at first and he was frightened. Not just terrified, but horrified. I heard them whisper that he came from the future. That the object, *The Mead*, a time traveling machine, had worked. At that time they said that they had to cover their tracks and must kill the dark-haired one before others came. They said they would be sending him to me, the Death Watcher.

XI
Stephen

"How do I get to him?" I said slowly as I approached the storekeeper.

He could tell by the seriousness in my eyes that I would hurt him very badly if he didn't tell me.

"I don't know, but I know someone who does," he said quickly.

"Who?"

"Archel!"

"The Archangel is still alive?" I said in complete awe and horror.

"Yes, and I can take you to him. We must hurry."

The storekeeper had me put on a Nazi uniform and we traveled through the night to Archel's home. I was going to Michel Archel's home: The Archangel. How could he still be alive? How could he still be in Germany? He was responsible for sending thousands of Jews to the gas chamber. I was terrified and even more horrified that David was at the hands of this monster.

We arrived at a small but quaint home. The porch light was on. The storekeeper knocked on the door. I heard a very low sound of someone stirring and coming to the door.

"Who is it?" The voice of an elderly man said.

"It is Hanz Stahl!" The storekeeper said.

"Who?"

"Hanz Stahl!"

"I don't know a Hanz."

"It is Sheep, Colonel. It is Sheep."

I stood behind the door as the old man opened it. He was surprised to see the stor-Sheep.

"Sheep? What are you doing here?" He said as I quickly pushed my way into his house.

"Waldouf!" He yelled in terror as he saw me, and then ran to his drawer to grab a gun.

I knocked it out of his hand, grabbed him by his collar, and started yelling at him. "HOW DO I GET TO DAVID? TELL ME HOW TO GET TO DAVID! WHERE IS HE?"

"Get away from me!"

"Stop it!" Sheep yelled at me and I threw Archel down in a chair.

"Tell us how it works, Colonel, and we will leave in peace," Sheep said.

"I don't know what you're talking about," he hissed. "And besides, I need to finish the little queer."

I leaped upon Archel. Archel screamed. "Tell us!" I broke one of Archel's fingers.

"AAAAH! SHEEP, HELP ME!"

"TELL US!" I screamed as I broke another finger.

Archel began to whimper.

"I'll hurt you worse. Now tell me how to get to David."

"Tell him, Colonel, and he won't hurt you anymore."

"Turn the bottom half of the Mead to the right and it re-sets. Now go away!"

Sheep and I left the house quickly and stood in the front yard.

"There's a car hidden a mile away from camp on the west side. The keys are under a big brown rock. It is the only rock there that color. When you arrive at camp, tell them you bring news of the Allies. There are some maps underneath my desk. Go quickly and save your friend."

"Aren't you coming with me?"

"No," he said quietly.

"Why?" I looked at him suspiciously.

"Tonight, I will be Sheep no more," he said dryly while I stared at him. "Go. Go save your friend."

I rushed quickly back to the store, leaving Sheep to whatever fate he had in mind for The Archangel.

XII
The Archangel

This one didn't scream. He fascinates me. He doesn't scream. I've used my worst techniques on him, but he doesn't scream. I like it. I like the silent terror in his eyes as I exact my punishment on him. An officer came running in.

"Colonel Archel. A Lieutenant Waldouf is here to see you. He brings word of the Allies. We must do away with this one quickly, Colonel. Now! The time is now. Sheep has gathered the Jews and prepared the chambers. Bring him quickly," said the officer.

"Ah. I need to finish, but it is getting complicated. Take him to the chambers now."

The officer gathered David's half-conscious body and drug him toward the gas chambers. Afterward, the new lieutenant had come. It seemed to Archel they were getting younger each time they came.

"Hail Hitler!"

"Hail Hitler!" Stephen said. "I bring news of the Allies. They are moving closer to the Rhine as we speak."

"This is not good. Lieutenant-"

"Waldouf. Stephen Waldouf."

"Lieutenant Waldouf, tell your superiors that we are right

on schedule. If there is a need, we will shut down the camp and come to our superiors' side. What is in that bag?"

"It is just personal items for tonight's stay. And how are the annihilations coming?"

"We are about to send a load to their God now. Come-"

An alarm went off. Someone was trying to escape.

"The fools! Excuse me, Waldouf. The chamber is that way."

XIII
Stephen

"Please God, let me get to him," I prayed aloud while I rushed down the halls toward the death chamber.

XIV
David

I was half-clothed lying on a cold floor. There were naked people surrounding me. They reached for me to help me up and some were crying hysterically. Where was I? My head ached and I couldn't see out of one eye from the beating. I barely stood up. The room was swirling and there were hundreds of naked people gathered close by. "It is the last shower!" Someone yelled out. *OH, GOD*, I thought to myself, *IT WAS THE GAS CHAMBER!*

XV
Young David

He was coming toward me slowly with that thing in his hand. It made a chilling scraping sound that got louder as he got closer. I couldn't move. Then someone started talking to me from far away. She said, "Scream, David, Scream!" I couldn't tell if it was Sophie or Mom, but I screamed as loud as I could.

XVI
Stephen

I was getting closer. There was a little man with dead eyes who was opening up the door to the chamber. I could smell the gas as it permeated the air. It was a pungent smell combined with a mixture of death and feces. I slowly walked into the chamber. There were hundreds of lifeless bodies lying everywhere. I tried to move one to look for David, but there were too many. I started to cry.

XVII
David

Stephen. Where was Stephen? I never told him I loved him! I wanted to scream. I needed to scream. "STEPHEN! STEPHEN! STEPHEN!"

XVIII
Stephen

I heard David, I heard David. I grabbed my bag and rushed out. The little man was about to close another gas chamber's door. I shot at him and he scurried away. I went inside the chamber and found David's bruised, bloodied body on the ground. I grabbed him up quickly. I opened the bag and retrieved the brown object. Someone yelled, "TAKE US WITH YOU!" I stopped and looked at all of them. Death was staring them all in the face. "I'm sorry. You're already dead," I said. They started to whimper. I reset the brown object and pushed the red button.

XIX
Young David

I never heard Wallace and the police officer break down the

door. I never heard the officer fire a shot at my dad as he lifted the axe toward me. I never heard my father scream and fall to the ground. I never heard the ambulance or the other police cars arrive. I never heard anything. I only remember being cradled in Wallace's arms as he carried me to safety. It was a feeling of warmth that I had not felt since Mom died. It was a feeling of home.

XX
Stephen and David

They arrived back at the thrift store in the basement. Stephen held David while he grabbed a blanket and wrapped it around him. He sat down in a chair that was in the middle of the floor and cradled David. He rocked his semiconscious body back and forth.

"Please don't leave me. Please don't leave me, David."

He said a silent prayer to God that he would be patient with David and that he wouldn't push or prod him about his past. He prayed that he would wait for time to be kind.

"Just let him live," he whispered while holding him close. "Please God, let him live."

David slowly looked up and noticed Stephen was crying. With a busted hand, he reached up and wiped away one of Stephen's tears. With slow deliberation, he reached up and kissed Stephen slowly and deeply. "Hold me," he said. Stephen held him closer and promised to never ever let go.

The End

TO FIND GOD IN ME

She asked me to find God in her. She asked me to find God through our lovemaking, through marriage, through childbirth, through our deaths. I could not oblige. I had to find Him. I had to search the corners of this Earth and find Him. I savored her kiss and tears as I said goodbye. She could not go on my journey. I was searching. I was searching for God.

I've seen many strange things and places. People would ask me what I sought and when I told them, they would take me to lost corners of their communities and show me their interpretation of God. Sometimes it would be a show by the local medicine man or woman which included a trick with a rock or stone, but every once in a while there would be an oddity that I could not explain or deny the mysticism of; however, it was not enough.

All my life I had heard of strange phenomena throughout the world: the little girl who cried holy oil or the sightings of Mother Mary on walls, tree trunks, rocks, or even in food. These were not the things I sought. I sought His voice. I sought a question. I sought an answer. I've come to the last corner of the Earth. Here, I may find my way.

It was a community near the Himalayas. A strange man took me to a boy who said he had seen God. He said the boy knew of a stairway to His Omniscience. I gave him a couple hundred dollars and he showed me the way. The boy, just an ordinary boy, took me to some steps at the beginning of a mountain. The steps had been beautifully placed steps on the mountainside. He told me to go and climb and I will find God. I started my ascent. I will not turn back no matter what.

The climb is monotonous, one-step, next step, all the same. I see no one. I hear no one, only the howl of the wind. I climb higher and higher as the air around me becomes colder, crisp, and foggier. I still won't turn back. I will find my way to His un-yielding righteousness and unflinching truth. I won't turn back even though the cold is cutting through to my bone. I won't turn back. Higher and higher I climb, searching for Him. There are thousands of steps before me, I decided to sit down and rest for a minute. The air is permeated with ice. I close my eyes and try to remember her. I try to remember her smile, her taste, her love, but the love is clouded by the many snowflakes that fall on me as I rest. *I'm so sleepy. It's so cold. I'll just close my eyes for a second and rest.*

The End

MRS. PETERSON AND THE PREACHER

I was rich. Filthy rich. I had married well and my husband had left me a huge fortune. This also left me prey to many scam artists and men who wanted to marry me for my money. Someone always wanted something from me. Always. Who could I trust? I was in a position of power, wealth, and achievement. I was used to it by now, but it left me lonely and afraid to commit to anyone and anything. I began to live in an isolated world full of servants and beautiful items. The servants were afraid of me and the items were cold, but such is the life of the wealthy.

My servant, Marie, was looking out the window. There were two young women approaching my doorstep. How they got past security, I will never know.

"I think they Jehov witness," Marie said in broken English.

"I'll take care of this, Marie," I said. Before they could reach the doorstep, I grabbed my purse and pulled a fifty from it. I went to the door, opened it before they rang the doorbell, and thrust the fifty toward them. "Here." They looked at me with blank smiles on their faces and then they turned and smiled at each other. They were pretty young girls. One was dressed in a pink shirt and white pants and the other was wearing a t-shirt that said, "Such is the power" with a pair of blue jeans. They didn't look like Jehovah's Witnesses. They just looked like kids. The one in the pink shirt looked back at me, smiled again, and said, "Thank you for your kind generosity. It will go toward a good cause." And they left. I thought that was weird, but a fifty was worth not hearing all that religious rubble.

"You should not give," Marie said. I turned and she was standing there with a look of concern. "They come back when you give."

"Oh Marie, stop being such a worrywart. Go do something," I said a little irritated. She left quickly, but she still had a look of concern on her face. Marie was the youngest of my servants. She was quick to make a comment when it wasn't called for. I should have fired her a long time ago, but I attributed her outbreaks to her youth.

My. That was the most excitement I've had in weeks, I thought to myself. I had quit the breakfast club. It usually consisted of rich old widows who talked constantly about their jewels, furs, and expensive collectibles. I found it boring. I mean, how many times can you hear about Benjamin Franklin's monocle? Still, I wondered if I had isolated myself from the world and I wondered if I was becoming one of those old eccentric widows that you read about in an Agatha Christie's novel. I sometimes longed for someone or something different to come into my world, but it hadn't happened for many, many years. "I'm tired. I think I'll lie down until lunch," I said to myself. I did that a lot. Its age, I told myself- only age.

I slept for several hours and was awakened by the doorbell. There appeared to be an argument brewing downstairs. I went out quickly and came to the top of the stairs. Marie was arguing with James, my butler.

"Burn it!" Marie was saying.

"This is for Mrs. Peterson," the butler said with irritation in his voice.

"Burn it! Bad! It's bad! No good for Ma'am," Marie said frightened.

"For heaven's sake, Marie! You're superstitions!" He said impatiently.

"What is it?" I yelled from atop the stairs.

"Don't!" Marie whispered loudly.

"You have a letter, Mrs. Peterson, from a Reverend Hanson. It was delivered by two young ladies."

"I told you not to give. They bad," Marie said.

I walked down the stairs quickly.

"Marie, *please*. Do something. Go! Go!" I said waving her off. She was about to say something else. "Now!" I said then stared at her until she left.

"I don't know why you put up with her," My aggravated butler said.

"Where's the letter, James?" I asked.

"Here you are," he answered then waited until I opened it.

"Thank you, James," I said. I looked at him impatiently and he walked away quickly.

I went into my study and sat down at my desk. The letter was a sealed envelope and it had a strange but pleasant smell to it. It had an unusual impression on the seal. I had to admit I was a little excited. *This is starting to be such a strange day.* It was a somewhat welcome change, however. I opened the letter and it read:

Dear Mrs. Peterson,

Yes. I know your name. Sarah and Mary told me how generous you were to them. Let me assure you that the money you gave will go to a very good cause. I have a religious community here where we worship God in a loving and caring environment. Your simple donation will help bring school supplies to our precious children for another week. We self-teach our children and they have had top-rated performances on the state mandated tests. Our children are happy and well adjusted.

As the leader of this community, I have the awesome responsibility of taking care of everyone. I have to make sure they are well fed, healthy, and receive appropriate shelter. I do love my job, but there are days when I just want to be me. I don't know if you can understand what I'm saying. Just the simple act of going to a Coke machine can be daunting at times. I don't mean to sound ungrateful. I am the luckiest man alive to be surrounded by so much love. I would just like to sit and have a conversation with someone who doesn't want anything from me.

Let me remind you again that I'm the luckiest man alive. The love everyone shows me swells my heart on a daily basis. I have to be honest. I enjoy being a mother hen. I enjoy taking care of my little community. I guess its part of my upbringing. I was the older brother to three siblings whom I had the responsibility of taking care of. I don't know what else I can do. I don't know what else I would do. I hate to be informal, but I love my job.

Mrs. Peterson, I invite you to come to our little community. I would like to have a personal conversation with you. Sit with me. Walk with me. Tell me of your life and your loves. It would be a personal blessing to me.

Take I-35 to Waxahachie and exit at Nederland. Take a right and go down until you see our sign, "Baton Community." Make a left and come up to our community. Someone will direct you to me. I look forward to seeing you.

Cordially,

Rev. Jonathan Hanson

What a personal letter, I thought to myself. *Why does he presume I'll come? He doesn't know me.* Still I was awed by this whole ordeal. Why not go? I wasn't doing anything. I hadn't done anything in years, yet and still he was a stranger. You always hear about these religious communes in the newspaper, particularly the ones with the leaders supposedly sleeping with young children. Still, I didn't think a religious pervert would be concerned about state test scores. He interested me that I had to admit. I, too, was an older sibling. Where he found joy in his responsibility, I found being the oldest tiring and cumbersome. "What would it hurt if I go?" I said aloud. I'd be sure to take the chauffeur with me so I wouldn't be alone. "James!" I yelled. "James! Draw my bath."

An hour later, I was dressed in my form fitting pink dress. Surprisingly at my age I still had a figure. I didn't know who I was trying to impress—me, an old lady, but I felt giddy to meet this man. Charles was getting the limousine ready. He carefully drove around to pick me up at the front door. I got into the limo when Marie came running out the front door hysterical.

"Don't go, Ma'am! Please don't go," she pleaded. "Bad people! Bad."

I rolled down the window and said, "Marie, go into the house! I've had enough of your outbreaks. We will have a serious conversation when I return. Charles, let's go," and we drove off.

"But you won't return," Marie said as a tear rolled down her cheek.

The drive was a pleasant one. The air was cool and the sky was cloudy with a few rays of sunshine shining through. Charles turned down Nederland and we were on our way to Jonathan's community. I anticipated meeting him. I wondered if he was handsome. He sounded so charming in his letter. I felt like a schoolgirl. It was a good feeling, but I had to be realistic, *I'm old and men are seldom attracted to old women.* All I could hope for was to be a mother figure, which wasn't so bad. Better still, a friend. Yes, a friend would be much better. I could talk to a friend. He wanted to know my life and my loves. No one has thought about my life or my loves for such a long time.

I could see the "Baton Community" sign in the near distance. "Almost there," I whispered to myself. Charles turned into the commune. The place was bustling and everyone stopped and turned as we drove up. Children came running to the limo as if it were a flying saucer. Charles got out of the limo and came around to my side and opened the door. We stood there as the children were looking at us in wonderment. I got out to "Ooohs" and "Ahhhs" from the children. A friendly looking man came up to us.

"Hi. Welcome to Baton. I'm William. How can I help you?"

"I'm here to see Reverend Hanson. He invited me," I replied.

"Of course. Come on down. You folks hungry? We're about to have supper. Kids! Kids! Get away from that car," he yelled. The children scattered and began to play. Charles and I walked with the man to a small building. He stopped and called, "Reverend Hanson? Reverend Hanson?"

"Yes, William?" A tall man answered while coming out the door.

"You have visitors," William said. Rev. Hanson looked straight at me and smiled. I blushed a little. He was awfully handsome with dark hair and green eyes.

"Are you Mrs. Peterson?" He asked.

"Yes, I am, and this is Charles, my chauffeur."

"Welcome. Welcome to the both of you," he said joyfully. "Are you hungry, Charles? Of course you are. William, take Charles to the Mess Hall and get him some food." Charles looked at me and I motioned to him that it was Okay. They walked off together. Jonathan turned to me and smiled, "Mrs. Peterson, it is such a pleasure to have you here. We seldom have visitors. Are you hungry?"

"A little," I said.

"Well, we'll be happy to get you something to eat, but first walk with me. I want to show you what use we have made of your donation."

We walked a little ways and there was this simple iron

building with plenty of windows. "This is our school house. Come inside," he said. Inside there was a lady working diligently at her desk.

"Sharon?" He said as she looked up. "This is Mrs. Peterson. She made a donation to our community." Sharon smiled, stood, and came toward us.

"Oh, thank you. Thank you so much," she said while shaking my hand.

"You're welcome," I said blushing. "It was only fifty dollars."

"Now, now, Mrs. Peterson, no donation is too small. Each and every penny is welcomed here. Sharon, show Mrs. Peterson what you're working on. Sharon graduated Magna Cum Laude from the University of Texas."

"Do you have to tell everyone, Reverend?" She asked blushing. Jonathan began to laugh. He had a hearty laugh.

"Of course I do," he said playfully.

Sharon rolled her eyes and said, "Whatever. I'm working on teaching the kindergarten class algebra."

"Algebra? Aren't they too young for that?" I asked.

"You're never too young. It sounds complicated but I'm using teddy bears and puppies to explain negatives and positives. It's an experiment, yes, but I hope they can get a grasp of it before they reach the elementary level."

"I'm impressed," I said.

"Sharon is quite a jewel to our community. Come now, Mrs. Peterson. Let's get you something to eat. Sharon, we'll talk later."

"Nice to meet you," Sharon yelled after us.

I wondered if something was going on between the two of them.

As if Jonathan could read my thoughts he said, "Sharon

and her husband have two kids. They attend school with the rest of the children here."

"I see," I said, a little relieved.

"Here we are at the Mess Hall," he said while opening the door. The hall was filled with adults and running children. Everyone was talking and eating. They seemed happy and content. A few people looked up to see who I was, but then they went back to eating and enjoying their conversation. We sat at the head table and a couple of people brought bowls of stew and cornbread. "It tastes better than it looks," he said. He then bowed his head and said, "Oh Father and Leader of us all, thank you for your nourishment and thank you for the gift of Mrs. Peterson. Her presence here is a complete joy. Amen."

"Amen," I said. I started eating and found the stew as delicious as he said. I noticed that nothing seemed weird or out of place. Children played as usual. People conversed as if nothing was wrong. I got no ill vibes whatsoever. Jonathan seemed normal. Little kids would come up to him and he would pinch off a piece of cornbread and give them some. No one appeared to regard him as someone to worship or fear. Everyone just went about his or her business in a normal fashion. I told myself to give Marie a proper scolding when I got back home. We finished our meal and Jonathan asked me if I would like to see the rest of the commune. I said yes.

It was a small yet lovely place. People had planted flowers in different places to give it a homey look. Children came up to Jonathan and he offered them a kindly hug. "The children are my favorite part of this job," he said. Jonathan noticed that I was growing a little tired. "Here have a Coke with me." He put change in the Coke machine and brought forth two cans to drink. We sat on the porch and talked while we drank our Cokes.

"Why did you name this place Baton, Jonathan?" I asked.

"When I was a young man, I traveled a bit. I came across a girl in Baton Rouge who stole my heart in one night. Needless to say, she stole many men's hearts. I have to be honest, there are nights when I still think about Baton Rouge." He laughed that hearty laugh once again. "I'm being naughty, Mrs. Peterson. And what is your story?"

"I think you can read me a mile away, Jonathan. Lonely widow in search of something new to enhance her life," I said.

"You're more than welcome here, Mrs. Peterson. We can always use a helping hand," he said.

I looked around the place and noticed I didn't see Charles. "Where's Charles?" I asked.

"He must be on the other side of the community. They're probably offering him homemade cookies," he said smiling.

What a joy Jonathan was. In the little time I had spent with him, I could tell he was an at-ease person oblivious of his attractiveness. He was kind and offering in a gentle way. I looked around the commune and noticed things were settling down to a slow pace. Evening was slowly creeping upon us. I looked to the south and noticed a building on top of a hill. It's funny, but I hadn't noticed it before.

"What's that building, Jonathan?" I asked.

"It's our worship hall. Would you like to take a closer look?"

"Yes, I would," I replied.

We put our Cokes down and began to climb the small hill.

"It was the first building built in our little community," Jonathan said.

I don't know why, but I began to feel a little lightheaded. Jonathan continued to talk as we climbed the hill.

"The glass windows were decorated and handmade in Egypt. Aren't they beautiful?" He said smiling.

Blue eyes! His eyes are blue. I thought they were green, I thought to myself.

Jonathan seemed to be talking more slowly to me now.

"Our doors were hand carved in Italy," he said in a warped tone.

My head was swimming. Jonathan's eyes were black. They were black now. I began to get frightened. Something was wrong. I wanted to run, but Jonathan grabbed my hand and led me forward. "Just a little bit more," he said in a voice that sounded distant and deep. We came to the top of the hill in front of the worship hall and I noticed the windows were decorated with ghastly images. I looked at Jonathan and his eyes were red. His eyes were *red*. I tried to run, but he had a vice grip on my hand. "Mrs. Peterson?" He called. I wouldn't look at him. I tried not to look at him, but he was crushing my hand. I looked at him and his eyes were on fire. "Mrs. Peterson, I know where the soul is."

I screamed, then darkness.

Marie was sleeping in her bed. She tossed and turned and awakened abruptly, breathing hard. She sat up in bed and looked around the room alarmed, but nothing was there. She lay in her bed again resting on her pillow. She could not sleep and decided to look at the ceiling. The moonlight played tricks with the curtain casting frightening images on her ceiling. She could hear the wind blow against her window taking leaves and debris to unknown places. She wanted her mother very badly, but she didn't know why. *Things seem terribly wrong tonight,* she thought to herself. The moon was too bright, the wind too noisy. There was a scratching, scraping sound at her window. *It's probably the wind,* she thought to herself. *Or was it?* She wanted to get out of her bed to check the window, but she was hesitant. She did not know what was out there. The scraping was a little louder this time. *Go to Lupe's room*, she thought to herself, *just go to Lupe's room.* She got out of the bed and went to the window. She saw nothing. She went back to bed.

Marie awoke abruptly again. She heard the whistling of the wind outside her window. Someone seemed to be calling her in the distance. They called to her again in a gravelly, wistful voice outside her window. Someone, no, something was out there. She grabbed her grandmother's crucifix. Her grandmother told her to always keep it near. She went to the window, pulled the curtain aside, and looked out. What was once Mrs. Peterson was now floating outside her window. It had a pasty, white face with fangs and claws where her hands used to be. Marie wanted to scream, but she didn't. This was her mistress. This was her employer. This was her friend.

"Come with me, Marie," Mrs. Peterson said in a whispery voice. "Join us."

"Go away!" Marie said frightened.

"We want to taste you, Marie. Let us taste you," Mrs. Peterson said.

Marie held up her grandmother's crucifix and the thing that was once Mrs. Peterson cowered then flew away. As it left, Marie wasn't certain, it may have been the moonlight playing tricks with her eyes, but she could have sworn she saw a tear running down the face of the thing that was once Mrs. Peterson.

"Goodbye, Mrs. Peterson," she said while letting a teardrop fall on her grandmother's crucifix. "Forever."

The End

I WANT TO LIVE

His chest rose up and down as he took slow deep breaths while sleeping. He let out a loud snore and I started to laugh.

"What's so funny?" He said, his body stirring awake.

"You make a funny face when you snore," I said.

"You're the best, Janice."

"Tell me again, Rodney," I said pulling him close to me.

"You're the best," he murmured and we started again.

I didn't want to face Mama. She always started in on me when I was away for a while. At seventeen, I was the only child of a mother who rarely smiled or enjoyed the pleasures of life. We were poor. Our apartment was littered with broken furniture that had had a joyous life in someone else's home. Mama tried to make our small apartment homey, but it came off as cheap-looking instead. She had plastic flowers everywhere- even on our kitchen table. God, they were butt-ugly but they were a part of her. Even today when I look at plastic flowers, it always reminds me of all the ass-whoopings I got as a child. I came in and she was sitting at the table.

"Where you been, girl?" She asked as she held a belt in her hands.

"I was down at the drugstore reading magazines," I lied.

"You been with that boy, Rodney?" She asked coming toward me.

"Nah, Mama! I haven't been with no one."

"I haven't seen no bloody rags this month, girl. You pregnant?" She said while raising a belt to me.

"No, Mama. Please don't whoop me." I was backing toward the door.

"You done got yourself knocked up messing with that old nasty boy."

"No, Mama. Please. Don't!" I screamed, but it was useless.

She began to hit me hard. Every lick was as painful as the next. I had to get out of there before she killed me. I ran to the subway and got on quickly. I don't know why, but riding the subway always gave me comfort. It reminded me of time traveling, taking me to a place of unknown journeys and curious destinations. Where it ended, I would never know. I listened as the metal wheels touched the rails. It hummed along toward an unknown future.

***

I couldn't believe I was still riding the subway. At thirty-nine, I was the youngest vice president of Newman Enterprises. One of the few Black vice presidents in this country, and I was still riding the subway. I guess it made me feel as if I was running away from something—what, I don't know. My stop was next. I grabbed my briefcase as if I had a million dollars in it. I had to in this city. You took nothing for granted. The minute you did was a minute you lost out. The doors opened, a cool breeze came in, and everyone rushed out of the car as usual. I headed straight to my job, which was in a high-rise on Twelfth Street. It was one of the prettiest buildings in the downtown area and I worked there. I was the fastest rising star of Newman Enterprises, a company that grossed 1.2 billion dollars last year. They've surpassed it this year because of me. I was headed toward the presidency. I was undaunted; nothing could stop me except for the unborn child I carried in my stomach.

Newman Enterprises was a conservative company with conservative values hidden behind closet affairs and clever mistresses. I fit like an anteater on an anthill. I knew the formula for success like the back of my hand. It came easy to me. Once I left Mama behind, it was like riding a lucky star, but this ride has developed worms lately, especially when the doctor said I was pregnant. I didn't know what to do. I told Samuel, my boyfriend of thirteen months. I never dreamed of his reaction.

"I'm not in this for babies," he said irately.

"It takes two to make a baby. We're not children," I said angrily.

"Then stop acting like one. You know what you have to do," he said while leaving my apartment. I haven't seen or heard from him since.

I walked to my building. The doorman recognized me at once and gladly opened the door for me. I went to the elevator as others gathered inside. It gave me a small thrill to see who was getting off on what floor. When I was the next to the last one left on the elevator, the other person getting off the elevator would always look back wondering where I was going. I was going to the top, because that's where I belonged. That's where I fit in and that's where I wanted to stay. It's where I needed to be. So, yes, I needed to stop acting like a child and do what had to be done, immediately.

I stepped off the elevator, said my usual good mornings, and headed straight to my office. My office was decorated with Louis XIV furnishings. It was old, classy, and expensive. I had a view of the park outside my window, which overlooked the downtown area. It was beautiful. The trees were sea green all year and you could smell honeysuckle touched by morning dew every day. I had a wine closet and a refrigerator filled with expensive cheeses and hors d'oeuvres that were supplied to me on a weekly basis. The closet in my office was filled with expensive suits designed for me to wear in an emergency or if I had a power lunch or meeting. My bathroom was decorated with gold fixtures and warm colors. The warm colors always reminded me of a comfortable place, of a home that I did not have growing up. It reminded me of summer. It reminded me of the few times I saw my mother laugh as a child. It was a warm and hearty laugh. There were days when I longed for that laugh. There were days when I needed that laugh to keep me going. When I needed to feel my mother, I just sat at my desk, closed my eyes, and reminisced.

The gold fixtures, in contrast, reminded me of the cold, hard business, which had surrounded my world. It was a world of shark bait and shark bite, and which one you were depended on your knowledge, charisma, and ability to stomp someone to a pulp—in a gentlemanly way, of course.

I had a headache. I told my secretary, Agnes, to hold my calls for an hour. I needed to call my doctor and make arrangements for the abortion. I needed time to do this. I took a couple of deep breaths and picked up the phone to dial my doctor. It rang once.

"Hello, Dr. Hunter's office," announced the nurse.

"Hello, April. This is Ms. Davis. Can I speak to Dr. Hunter?"

"Hello, Ms. Davis. I'll see if he's available."

A few seconds later, Dr. Hunter answered, "Hello, this is Dr. Hunter."

"Dr. Hunter, this is Janice Davis. I, uh, need to make arrangements for an abortion," I said nervously then took a deep sigh.

"Are you sure, Janice?"

"Yes, doctor, I'm sure."

"Let me check my schedule. Come see me Friday morning and we'll do the procedure here. You'll need to rest for a couple of days afterward," he said.

"Thank you, Dr. Hunter."

"Of course, Janice. Goodbye."

That was it, I thought to myself. It was simple. In a couple of days it would all be over and things would be back to normal.

When I finished at work, I headed straight to the subway. It had been a long day. Allen Richards, the president of the firm, was particularly anxious today. He said he was getting a new assistant tomorrow. *How long before he screwed her?* I thought to myself. Allen was infamous for his behavior. He often asked his attractive female employees for sexual favors. I quit counting the times he asked me. He was mostly harmless except to his new assistants who were usually young, naïve, and gorgeous. He would have them eating out of his hands before their first week was up. Eventually, he would tire of them and ask them to do some work for which they were ill qualified then use that as an excuse to fire them.

The subway wasn't crowded today, but I felt like standing up on the way home. I don't know why, I just did. The lights would lower as we entered the tunnels and brighten as we left them. It felt like traveling through time. I closed my eyes and remembered.

***

Mama was going to kill me, I thought to myself. She's right; I hadn't had a period this month. Some of the people in the subway car were staring at me. I looked a mess. My hair was tousled and my clothes needed to be adjusted. I was trying not to cry. What am I going to do? I should have been more careful. I just wanted Rodney so much. We had met at the drugstore near my apartment. I was looking at a bridal magazine when he walked up to me and told me I would look beautiful in the bridal gown I was staring at. He asked me to take a walk with him. I was hesitant at first until he smiled the warmest smile I had ever seen. He was so kind and playful and seemed to understand me. He listened to my stories of how badly I wanted out. And I desperately wanted out. Then, when he said he wanted to make love to me, I thought the whole world lit up. I didn't take time to think about protection. I just wanted him at that moment and I didn't want anything to stop us. And now I didn't know whom to turn to. The only other family I had was my mama's sister, Aunt June. Maybe she would know what to do. She had everything. Maybe she'd help.

Aunt June stayed in the expensive part of town. She didn't come to our side even though she was from there. She had two daughters, Thelma and Sherry, and they were in college already. They grew up with all the privileges of the well to do and were snobbish and uppity. They always bragged about their material things. They would offer me clothes and items at times, but they always made me feel like they were giving to the downtrodden and the needy. I knocked on her door. It was a wooden door, hand-carved. Beautiful. She answered, "Janice? Janice! What's wrong?"

"I think I might be in trouble." I could barely hold back my tears. I could have sworn I caught a wry smile on Aunt June's face.

"Come in, darling," she said while leading me to the dining room. Her house was filled with expensive furnishings that had a "do not touch" aura about them. She led me to a long, exquisite dining table and chair set. I could smell meat cooking from the kitchen. I didn't know how hungry I was until I smelled her food. I wanted some, but she did not offer any. We sat down at the table.

"What's wrong, Janice?" She asked softly with a look of anticipation in her eyes.

"I think I might be pregnant," I said hesitantly.

"Oh, dear, you've been doing something with a boy?"

"Yes," I said quietly with my head down.

"What does his family do?" She asked while lifting my face.

"He don't have no daddy. His mama lives off the government," I said. I noticed another slight, wry smile on Aunt June's face.

"Oh, dear, I don't know what I would do if Thelma or Sherry came home pregnant? I'm just glad they're away in college building a life for themselves," she said sighing.

"What can I do?" I asked.

"Have you talked to your friend about this?"

"No."

"Well, talk to him, honey, and buy one of those pregnancy tests. Call me and let me know the results," she said.

I heard a little timer go off in the kitchen. Aunt June immediately rose from the table.

"Now, Janice, let yourself out. I have things I have to do. Don't worry, everything will be all right. Talk to your friend and have a cookie on the way out." She said as she disappeared into the kitchen.

It sounded like she emphasized "a" when she said, "Have a cookie." I got "a" cookie on the way out. I started to leave it, but I was very hungry. It tasted sweet and buttery in my mouth. I noticed Aunt June hadn't offered me anything else to eat and didn't offer to pay for my pregnancy test either. She knew I didn't have the money. It was a funny thing about the elite. They would help a person with a million dollars in the bank but wouldn't help a poor person in their own family. She and her family were the "haves" in our family and we were the "have-nots." Her people were never mean or detached and no one ever said anything hurtful. It was just the subtle things, like not being included for the picture taking or at meals: little indiscreet things that reminded us that we were not part of their world.

I hated my life. It was a poor life with not enough food, not enough clothes, not enough shoes, and not enough love. Aunt June made me feel beneath her. She made me feel like a burden, a nuisance, a fly, and a nothing. Why did the "haves" have to do that? Why couldn't they reach back and care enough to bring the poor with them? Aunt June needed to feel above us and that made me sad. It also made me angry enough to want to get out. It made me determined to find a way out of the hole I was living in. I needed to talk to Rodney. We would find a way out together. We would find enough, especially enough love. I walked to the subway and got on. I stared ahead into the tunnels and it somehow felt like I was dropping into another world. *A better world* I hoped, I prayed, I begged. The subway made a swooshing sound, taking me to a place of uncertainty.

***

I was late for work and barely made it to the station this morning. The subway was particularly crowded. People were pressed very close to me. For an instant, I thought about the safety of the baby, but that quickly went away. I knew what must be done and there was no stopping me. I let my mind wander to Allen's new assistant. Would she be some dainty little blonde like the last one or would she be a smoldering brunette with legs as long as a giant grasshopper? It was a common joke around the office: "How long will this one last?" or "Has he laid her yet?" someone would ask. I'd even taken bets on some of them. I'd already won two hundred dollars. I laughed to myself as the subway came to a stop. I walked carefully out of the car, trying not to bump into anyone.

The doorman let me into the building with a smile as usual. I went quickly to the elevator and we all did our floor routine. I was the last one left on the elevator, of course. I walked quickly to my office and stopped to gossip with Agnes, my secretary.

"Well?" I asked with a tone that insisted on an answer.

"She's Black, pretty, and she reminds me of someone."

"She's Black? Oh, Allen has a taste for chocolate this month," I said laughing.

"Now you know we're being messy," Agnes said and started laughing. "Hey, meeting in five minutes," she added.

I quickly went into my office, grabbed my file, notepad, and pen. Checked my makeup and hair, and left. I walked down the hallway in anticipation.

I saw them standing at the end of the hallway. I don't know why, but I felt a sense of foreboding as I walked closer to them. Allen was talking to the new girl. I could see she was petite in size with shoulder-length hair. I wanted to run away from them, but I didn't know why. As I got closer, my heart seemed to weigh a thousand pounds. I wanted to leave, but I couldn't. Allen smiled at me and motioned for me to come closer. I walked up to them and then I saw her. I had stared into those eyes a million times. I just stood there staring at her.

"Janice, this is Kimberly. Kimberly Davis, my new assistant," he said proudly.

I said nothing.

"Hi, how are you doing?" She said in a friendly tone.

"Hey, you two look alike. Are you kin? You both have the same last name," Allen asked.

"No," I said quickly.

I was just staring at her. They both were starting to feel uncomfortable. Allen broke the silence by saying, "Hey, it's time for the meeting." I walked silently behind them down the hall. Allen tried to slice through the tension by making small talk. We entered the boardroom and I sat down quickly. Everyone noticed my anger, but they didn't say a word. Allen introduced Kimberly to everyone. They were pleased to meet her. No one dared to comment on her resemblance to me for fear of my retaliation. Everyone knew my silence meant frustration.

Before the meeting started, Allen proudly and loudly asked Kimberly to take minutes of the meeting in shorthand. She produced a pad and pen and nodded a smile toward Allen to begin the meeting. I hated that smile. I hated her. What was Allen trying to pull, hiring someone who looked like me? What type of psychological game was he playing? He'd always wanted to sleep with me, but this was ridiculous. I was sitting at the table in a state of pure resentment. Bill Sunder, the head of Sales, noticed my discomfort and fidgeting.

"Janice, would you like a cup of coffee?" Bill asked.

"Yes, please," I said sighing.

"Ms. Davis, would you get Janice a cup of coffee?" Bill said.

"Of course," she said pleasantly.

Kimberly got a steaming cup of coffee and walked it over to me. I tried not to look at her while she was handing it to me, but we collided and the hot coffee spilled on my hand and burned me.

"Oh, I'm so sorry," said Kimberly, embarrassed while backing away.

"WHAT KIND OF IDIOT ARE YOU?" I screamed while rising out of my chair. "YOU CLUMSY FOOL!"

"Janice, it was an accident," Allen said while coming quickly to my aid. Bill was wiping up the spilled coffee.

"YOU HIRED THIS INCOMPETENT!" I screamed.

"Janice, that's enough!" Allen was beginning to get angry.

"SHE BURNED ME! I'M GOING TO THE HOSPITAL!" I screamed as I left the meeting.

I ran to my office. Agnes was standing at her desk with a look of concern. "Janice, what's wrong? What happened?" She asked as I whisked past her. I grabbed a napkin full of ice, then my purse, and rushed out. Agnes called after me, but I headed straight to the elevator, ignoring her. *She did that on purpose*, I thought to myself. *I'm going to get her,* I said in my head over and over. Who was she? Where did she come from? Why did I have such strong emotions toward her? Allen knew what he was doing when he hired her. A younger version of me; it was sick. He was playing such a sick game. I headed straight to the subway. I listened to the subway car as it whistled to a stop. I got on quickly. It whistled on its way toward my home. I could see the past as the shadows crept by.

***

I was looking for Rodney everywhere. I finally asked old man Hawkins, who sold cassettes, CDs, and God knew what else on the corner. He usually knew everything. He said Rodney was down in the Staple Building. I ran to him. The Staple Building was old, very old. It housed the elderly and several families. The tenants there stayed to themselves while the drug dealers tended to their drug business. The dealers usually hung out in front of the building or on the stairwells. They all had a crude look to them. They were dead serious and had soulless eyes.

I went inside the building and started yelling for Rodney. "Stop that racket, girl," someone yelled out. "Rodney's on the roof," someone else called out. I briefly wondered why Rodney was here in this building, but I had bigger problems facing me. I ran up the stairs. People were staring at me. I ignored them. I opened the door to the roof. I looked out and there was Rodney standing next to some guy. He was giving Rodney something. Rodney put it in his pocket then slapped the man's hand in gratitude. I called to Rodney. They both looked startled as I came toward them. The man with Rodney looked apprehensive. Rodney motioned to him that it was okay.

"Janice, what are you doing here?" Rodney asked angrily.

"I need to talk to you," I said flustered.

Rodney started toward me. "This is not a good time, Janice. Go home," he said while grabbing my arms and pulling me toward the door.

"Rodney, I think I'm pregnant."

He stopped and looked at me for what seemed like forever. He motioned for the man to leave. The man came up to Rodney. "It's okay, man. I'll catch up with you later," he said. The man quietly walked past me.

"Rodney, let's go away from here. Let's start a life together. We can make it. I know we can," I said to him while grabbing his hand.

He let go of my hand quickly and said, "You must be crazy. We got nothing. No money. No car. No home. We are nothing."

"We can do this, Rodney. I know we can," I pleaded.

"How, Janice, with no education and me slanging dope," he said irritated.

"You sell dope?" I said surprised.

"What else can a man like me do? I'm a nothing. You're a nothing. Look how we live, Janice. I don't want to bring a child into our world. It would be cruel. We're going to do something about this," he said while pulling me through the door then into the stairwell.

"Where are we going, Rodney?" I asked while being pulled down the stairs.

"My homeboy owes me a favor."

We came to a door on the next floor. He rapped on the door several times. A tall man with hollow eyes then held the door slightly ajar. "What is it?" He said.

"Open up, man. I need a favor," Rodney said while stepping into the man's apartment.

"Come on, Janice." Rodney said.

"What is this, Rodney?" I was beginning to become frightened.

Rodney left my side then went to the strange man and started whispering. Every moment or so they would turn and look at me. The man left and went into the back room. Rodney came toward me.

"Why are we here, Rodney?" I said hesitantly.

"He's going to fix this," Rodney answered.

"He's going to fix what?" I asked confused.

"He's going to fix our problem."

I then realized what Rodney was talking about. "No, Rodney! I won't do it!" I shouted while Rodney grabbed my arm.

"What else you gonna do? I'm not going to be here for you. I won't be there for you," he said and released my arm.

"Then I'll raise it by myself. I won't kill it," I said and backed away from him.

"And how long before you become your mother?" He said slowly.

I stopped dead in my tracks.

"How long before you get old eyes, Janice? How long before

you lose your soul? How long before you start hating it? We have nothing to give it, Janice. Nothing!"

I started crying. I thought of the empty mother I had at home. I wondered what she would have been if I hadn't been born. I wondered if she'd ever smile, laugh, or just enjoy the sunshine. I didn't want to become like her. I never wanted to become like her. The tears were rolling hard down my cheeks. I took a slow step toward the back room. I looked at Rodney. "Nothing," he said with his head down as I took more steps past him. I entered the room. There was a long bed in the middle of the floor. A chair sat at the bottom of the bed.

"Take off your pants and wrap that sheet around you," the man said.

I took my pants off and got the sheet. I was surprised it was clean. "Lie on the bed and let the sheet cover you." I did as he said. The sheet dropped from side to side.

"I want you to scoot all the way down to the end of the bed with your bottom hanging and your legs open. You must be perfectly still and relaxed. Do you understand?" He asked coldly.

"Yes," I said quietly.

I did what he instructed. The man grabbed a long instrument and stuck it in me. The pain was excruciating, but I held still. In a moment, the child was taken from my body. He wrapped it up and put it somewhere. I didn't look where. I wanted to lie there and die, but the man told me to get up. "You will bleed for about a week," he said while handing me a sanitary napkin. "Take it easy for a couple of days." I slowly got dressed.

When I walked out of the room, Rodney was not there. I never saw him again. I walked home slowly. Mama was sitting in a chair waiting for me. "Where you been, girl?" She said without getting up. "I just went for a walk, Mama. I don't feel very good.

I'm going to lie down," I said weakly. I don't know why, but all Mama said was a whispered "Okay" as I walked past her to my room. I never knew if she realized what I had done. She never said a word about it. I think she knew though. I lay in my bed for a few days then I got up and went to school the following week. A couple of months later, I finished high school and attended college upstate.

When I left Mama, I said I would never come back to that place. I would beg Mama to come see me, but she never did. She died soon afterward, during my sophomore year. I came home one more time to gather her things, but there was nothing worth saving. There was nothing worth cherishing. I left the apartment and headed to the subway to return to college. I could see my neighborhood pass by me like a flurry of ghetto postcards. I would never return there. For the first time in a long time, I thought about Rodney and the baby I had aborted. It would have been going on two by now. I didn't ask the tall man what it was, but somehow I knew what it was. It was a girl and I would have called her Kimberly. Kimberly Davis.

***

When I got home, I was fuming. My hand was still stinging. I got some more ice to put on it. I thought about how I was going to get that little bitch for burning me. I decided to just go to bed for now. I tossed and turned all night long. I kept having a bad dream that I couldn't remember. The next morning I called in sick. I knew what I was going to do. I was going to stab the little bitch over and over. I dressed in black slacks and a black hooded sweater. I put a knife in my coat pocket and caught the subway to my job. I waited outside the building until her lunchtime. I hid until I saw her come out of the building and head toward the park. *Good*, I thought to myself. *I can get her in a secluded area and go to work on the bitch.* I followed her as she walked onto a secluded path in the park. I swore I could hear the ghosts of the beaten, the mugged, the raped, and the murdered as I followed her. She came to a large tree and stood there facing it. I walked up behind her slowly. She turned and looked at me. I had stared into those eyes a million times. I dropped the knife and started to cry. She looked at me with an understanding smile and said, "Hi, Mama." I quickly grabbed her and hugged her tightly. I knew. I knew. I didn't care how or why. I was just holding my daughter, my beautiful daughter. I kissed her mouth, her eyes, her eyebrows, and her cheeks, all over her face.

"I'm sorry," I said while holding her. "I'm so sorry."

"I have to go, Mama," she said.

"Noooo!" I said as she pulled away from me. "How? Why?" I asked crying.

"He called to me, Mama. He wants to live. Let my brother live, Mama," Kimberly said and then she disappeared.

I sat down by the tree and cried. I cried for the loss of my job. I cried for being alone in the delivery room as I gave birth to my son. I cried for the first time he left my side to attend school. I cried for his graduation day from college. I cried for holding my first grandchild. And I cried for the silent tears my son would shed at my graveside. But mostly, I cried for my glorified Father who would allow me into heaven to see my beautiful daughter once again.

The End

THE STEP DAD

I hated him. Ever since he came into our lives, he has taken my mother away from me and I hated him for that. My name is Sonny and I'm eight and I have never had a father. It had just been my mom and me and I hated him for coming into our lives. My mom and I were so close. We did everything together. We shopped together, ate together, looked at TV together, played sports together, went to the Chucky Cheese together, and when the Closet Monster came to me and I became terrified, we slept together.

He came into our lives about a year ago. My mom seemed giddy like a little girl when she met him. She was so silly to me. She laughed and smiled a lot when he would come around. She started going on dates with him, leaving me with Grandma. I loved my Grandma but she wasn't Mom. We had fun together; it was a different kind of fun. It was fun with limits. I could only go so far with Grandma before she reeled in the serious look, which would knock me down a peg or two, but with my Mom I had lots of limits that I got away with. I guess that was the difference between parents and grandparents.

I missed Mom when she went on dates. It was as if a part of her was being taken away from me with each date she had with Dan. Yes, Dan, that's his name, but I like to call him Slimebutt, Stinkynose, and Cootyhead. Yes, that's what I like to call him. Mom would beg me to try to like him. She would sometimes cry when I said mean things about him, so I would try to be nice, but it would only last a little while and then I would start hating him again.   He tried to have a conversation with me, but it came off as awkward silence between us. I know he would rather I wasn't around, but I'm here to stay. She was my mom first and I'm not giving her up without a fight.

They want to talk to Grandma and me about something important tonight. Grandma is all excited, but I'm quiet. I think I know what it is and I'm terrified. He wants to marry my mom. I know it. I just know it. I want to cry so badly, but Grandma will scold me for not being nice about Cootyhead. It will never be the same again between Mom and me. I could just crawl away and die or let the Closet Monster take me down to his world. I don't think children return when they go to his world. I don't think they survive when they go to his world. I bet its dark and nasty down there, but right now it seems like a better place than this.

I could hear them driving up and getting out of the car. Mom has excitement in her voice that I can hear as she walks up the steps. The doorbell rings and my heart drops. Grandma rushes to open it. She whispers something and Mom says yes and they start dancing up and down. I want to die, just die. Cootyhead sticks his big nogging in the door and Grandma gives him a big hug. If I had a gun, I would have shot him. They're all celebrating and then they finally turn to me. Mom comes slowly over to me and tells me the news. She tells me Dan wants to marry her and that we're going to be a family. She says we're all going to live together. I ask her if she's happy and she says yes and she leaves me and goes back over to Grandma and Dan. I sit quietly watching them. I want to scream so badly, but I don't. I just run out of the room and slam the door real hard, leaving them in silence.

The next few months flew by in a whirl. Mom and Dan were married and he got a job in another state. We were moving out of state from Grandma. I was very sad about that and I left Grandma with my tears on her shoulder. Dan said we were moving into a big house. Mom was so excited and I was a little excited about that too. I had never had my own back yard and Dan promised to buy me a swing set. I was mostly concerned about the adventures I would have in my own jungle of a back yard. I hoped it would have a big tree so that I could climb up to the moon.

After a long drive, we drove up to the house and it was indeed big. It was a two-story home and it was beautiful. I looked up in awe at this big castle and I could only imagine the hiding places I would find. Mom started to cry and told Dan it was beautiful. Dan only gushed and rushed us inside to take a tour of our home. It had a big living room and a big kitchen. Mom screeched with excitement when she saw the kitchen. Dan opened the door to the back yard and I walked slowly toward it. I reached the door and stared in awe at the magnificent back yard. It had two trees, a small one and a big one. It also had a lovely rose bush and a big grassy knoll. It was heaven, heaven I tell you. Dan told me we could get a dog if I wanted one. I think I wanted to like him for that, but only for a little bit.

Mom called us upstairs. Her voice was full of excitement and Dan and I rushed upstairs. Their bedroom was massive with a big closet and a sunken tub in the bathroom. I couldn't wait to see my room and Dan and Mom walked me to it. It was much smaller than theirs, though bigger than I have ever had, but there was something off-center about the room. It had a cold, distant feel about it, which made a foreboding chill run up my spine. I told my mom I didn't like it. They both stared at me with a subdued curiosity mixed with disappointment. Mom bent down to me and said we just needed to fix the room up. Dan joined in and said they would buy me nice furniture that I could pick out. He then suggested we go get ice cream. I was glad for that. I wanted to be a thousand places other than in that room.

True to their word, they took me furniture shopping and I picked out what I wanted. I picked out blue furniture and Mom found curtains and a bedspread to match. I was a little excited when they brought the furniture home and Mom fixed up my room. It was a neat-looking room. Dan had bought me a poster of the "Toy Story" characters because that was my favorite movie. I told Mom to put it above my bed. I knew that Buzz Lightyear would protect me from everything, but the closet seemed to loom at me from time to time. I started staying mostly in the back yard. I loved the back yard and couldn't wait until Dan bought the swing set he promised.

One day I overheard Mom and Dan talking. They were concerned that I spent so much time in the back yard and not in my room. Dan told Mom that I was just an outdoors person and that they shouldn't be concerned, but Mom was still worried a little bit. I wanted to tell her that something's in my closet and it tries to get out at night, but I didn't dare. I was afraid that whatever was in there would get me for tattling. It scratches at the door sometimes and one day it's going to open it and take me away.

I haven't been sleeping well and Mom is starting to notice dark circles underneath my eyes. She and Dan sat me down and tried to talk to me about it, but I still wouldn't tell. Mom decided I would sleep with her and Dan for a couple of nights. Dan protested, but Mom said it would only be for a couple of nights until she could take me to the doctor. Their bed was nice and soft. I felt Dan stiffen when I got in beside them, but Mom was soft and cozy just like before he came into our lives. I slept straight through the night and even the next night too.

Mom took me to the doctor. I think I was more afraid of the doctor than the Closet Monster, but he turned out to be a very nice man. He asked Mom to wait out in the hallway for a little bit. He wanted to talk to me. He asked me what I was afraid of. I said nothing. He told me to fight my fears and fight whatever was hunting me because that was the only way to get rid of a Closet Monster. He knew about him. He knew, but I was too terrified to say anything. He gave me a lollipop and told me to sit outside while he spoke to Mom. He gave Mom a prescription and told her to give it to me as needed, but not every day because it was addictive. We left there and decided to go shopping. Dan would join us during his lunch break.

We came across an odd antique shop on our way to get burgers and Mom called Dan to meet us there. There was a mysterious woman behind the counter and she invited us to look around. There were exotic dolls and mystical whatnots all around. I could feel a presence in this shop, but I couldn't explain why. Dan walked in and Mom was glad to see him. He kissed her lightly on the mouth and I looked away. Dan started looking around the shop like a kid in a candy store. He was more excited than I was. I kept looking around and noticed that the mysterious woman was staring at me. She called to me and I walked to her. She told me in a low voice that I have much to fear and that I needed protection and then she slowly revealed a brown teddy bear. I started to laugh and told her I was too old for teddy bears, but she said this was a special teddy bear and that it had protected children for hundreds of years. I grabbed the teddy bear and instantly felt energy from it. I wanted it. I had to have it. I knew it would protect me against the Closet Monster. I called to Mom and Dan and they came over quickly. I told them I had to have this bear. Dan giggled a little bit and Mom shot him an angry look. Dan went to the counter and asked the woman how much it was. She told him three hundred dollars; Dan instantly got angry and said he wasn't paying three hundred dollars for an old teddy bear. She told him it was an antique and that it had protected many children for centuries. Dan offered her twenty dollars for the bear. She scoffed at his offer and became angry and asked us to leave her store before she called the police. We walked out of the store while Dan was mumbling curse words underneath his breath. We started toward the car and Mom fussed at Dan about his behavior. He only yelled that he'd buy me a stupid teddy bear and walked away from us going toward his office. We got in the car and Mom apologized for Dan's behavior. She also said three hundred dollars was a lot of money to pay for a toy. I sat there quietly on the way home knowing that that bear was my only hope against the Closet Monster. I was doomed.

Dan came home with a silly looking teddy bear for me as if I were a toddler. I just left it and went into my room. I could hear Mom and Dan arguing. Dan said Mom treated me like a baby and Mom yelled at Dan for being insensitive and told him not to make her choose between the two of us. Dan got very quiet at that statement and I heard Mom start to cry.

I went to bed and tried to get some sleep in my own room. I put a chair up against the closet door to keep the monster in. Mom wanted to give me a pill but I told her I was okay and I'd go to sleep on my own. The truth was I didn't want to cause any more problems for Mom. She looked very unhappy when she said goodnight. I fell asleep soundly until I heard the scratching at the closet door, but this time the scratching was louder. The monster tried the doorknob and became angry that he couldn't get through because of the chair. He shook the doorknob and pounded the door until the chair fell over. There was complete silence after the chair hit the floor. I lay there breathing hard with the covers up to my chin. Then there was a slow turn of the knob and the door slowly opened, pushing the chair to the side. I jumped from my bed and ran to Mom and Dan's room. Their door was locked. I started pounding on the door, but they wouldn't let me in. I could hear a loud scraping across my bedroom floor and I started screaming for Mom, but they wouldn't let me in. I could hear them arguing, but they wouldn't let me in. The scraping came to the entrance of my bedroom and then there was a blue curved slipper that stepped from the door as the door was slowly opening wide. I screamed and accidentally knocked my head against Mom's door then fell out in silence.

I dreamed I could hear Mom and Dan open the door and Mom scream. Dan said I was going into shock and they put me in a blanket and rushed me to the car. The next thing I remember was waking up groggy in the hospital. Mom was standing by the bed and Dan was holding her. The doctor was looking into my eyes with a light beam. He asked me how I felt and I told him my head hurt. He started asking me a bunch of questions like what state was I in, how old was I, and what year was this? I answered all of them correctly, but he told Mom and Dan that he'd feel better if I stayed overnight in the hospital for observation and they would do a brain scan in the morning. Mom wanted to stay with me but the doctor told her that "in her condition" she needed as much rest as possible. He said I would be all right and that the nurses would take good care of me. Dan said the doctor was right. Mom was hesitant at first, and then she finally agreed. She kissed me on my forehead and said she would be back in the morning. I didn't make a fuss. I just told her I'd be all right. I wanted to be far away from that thing in my room, but I wondered what condition my mom was in that she needed so much rest. I tried not to think about it and went to sleep.

The next morning I woke up and Mom was there. I smiled at her and gave her a big hug. I asked her why she didn't let me into the room. She said it was complicated and I wouldn't understand. I asked what does "in her condition" mean? She told me that we would talk about it later and that she wanted to know what I was so afraid of. I started looking down at my hands. She started begging me to tell her. I finally said "I can't, he'll get me." She sat very close to me on my bed and asked, "Who'll get you? Is it Dan?" I said no. I told her it was the monster in my closet and that it scratches at my door every night to get at me, but last night it came out of the closet and was going to take me down to his world. Mom looked serious and told me I've been talking about the Closet Monster for years. "This one is real," I told her. I also said, "He's going to get me if we don't go back home to Grandma." She started to say something, but the technician came in to take me for some fancy x-rays on my head. She told me we would talk about it later.

After the x-ray, the doctor said everything was fine and that I could go home. I was very quiet on the way home with Mom. When we got there, Dan came out with a big smile and said he had a big surprise for me. I got out of the car and walked in the house slowly. Dan was standing there with something behind his back. I looked at him curiously and Dan produced the teddy bear from the antique store. I could have jumped eight feet in the air. I grabbed the bear and started shouting, "I'm saved, I'm saved!" I shouted, "I'll get you now Closet Monster" and ran to my room. I sat on my bed for hours watching the closet with my teddy bear tucked safely in my hand until I fell asleep. I woke up to a rustling sound. I thought it was the Closet Monster, but it was Dan coming into my room in a rush. He told me to hurry and get dressed because Mom was bleeding and we needed to get her to the hospital before she loses the baby. We all quickly went to the hospital and Mom was put on a gurney and rushed into surgery. Dan and I stayed in the waiting room for a long time until the doctor came out and told us Mom and the baby inside her were okay and that she'd need a whole lot of rest. Dan asked if he could see her. The doctor said no because she was under sedation and wouldn't wake up until morning. He told Dan to go home and said both of us should get some rest.

Dan drove home in silence. He had nothing to say to me. I didn't know what to say myself. Mom was going to have a sister or brother for me and I knew Dan blamed me for Mom's complications. We got out of the car and walked into the house. I wasn't sleepy because I had taken a nap earlier, but Dan told me to go to bed. I went into my room and searched for the teddy bear. He was on the side of my bed, safe and sound. I looked into his ageless eyes and I could see a thousand smiling children laughing and playing so I hugged him tightly. He was going to save me from the Closet Monster, but I didn't know how. I started missing Mom an awful lot and hoped she really was okay. I didn't know how I felt about having a brother or sister, but I hoped they were okay too. I put the teddy bear down and went to Dan and Mom's room. Dan was sitting on the bed holding something cupped in his hand and a glass of water. He looked very angry and started yelling at me that it was my fault that Mom was in the hospital with complications. Then he said, "Take this sleeping pill and go to bed." He walked toward me with the pill and glass of water. I told him that I wouldn't be able to fight the Closet Monster if I took that pill. He started yelling even louder that there was no Closet Monster and that he would spank me if I didn't take the pill. I took the pill and drank the water then Dan yelled at me to go to bed. I walked back to my bedroom slowly. How was I going to fight the Closet Monster if I was in a deep sleep? I could only hope the teddy bear would fight for me. I tried to fight the sleep for a long time but the pill started working. I lie underneath my covers and fell asleep with my teddy bear grasped tightly in my hand.

I don't know what happened until the time I awakened, but I can only take a guess. Dan sat up in his room for a very long time fuming and feeling bad about Mom until he heard a slight noise coming from my room. Angrily, he marched toward my room, opened the door, and came face to face with the Closet Monster who was gathering me up to take me down to his world. The Closet Monster growled and Dan let out a loud scream. The monster then grabbed me up in my covers and quickly went into the closet. Dan yelled no and ran into the closet after me and we were transported down to the Closet Monster's world. In his world, the monster laid my unconscious body on an ancient table. He then chanted an old mystic incantation, and began inhaling the life force out of my body. You could see the aura coming from my body as he inhaled.

While this was occurring, Dan was lost in another part of the monster's world. He came down a cave-like entrance where there were children embedded in the cave wall, their limp arms protruding. Dan tried to walk quietly so that the embedded children wouldn't hear him, but he stepped on a twig and they immediately woke up and started screaming in unison. Their arms reached out to Dan trying to grab him, but Dan stayed out of reach until he came to an opening and saw me on the table with my life force being inhaled out of me. The monster stopped and growled at Dan while the embedded children grabbed him and wouldn't let him go. Dan tried to break free but couldn't and the monster started inhaling my life force once again. Dan started yelling for them to stop and I could hear him from far away as he tried to break free from the embedded children but they had a vice grip on him. I could hear Dan yelling, "Wake up, Sonny," but it was like hearing something in a distant canyon. The yelling came louder, closer. I could hear Dan clearly shouting, "Wake up, Sonny!" I started to awaken, and when I woke up, I came face to face with the Closet Monster. He had a gruesome face and very big sharp teeth that clenched together in an ugly grin. I let out a huge scream and tried to get away from the monster, but he grabbed my arm and started sucking the life out of me again. I could feel myself growing weak, but Dan was yelling, "Fight him, Sonny. Fight him!" I could feel myself growing weaker and weaker until I remembered the teddy bear in my other hand. I could hear Dan shouting from far away, so I hit the monster with my teddy bear. The Closet Monster recoiled in fear, so I hit him again. Whatever was happening, the embedded children were losing their grip on Dan and he broke free and ran to my side. Dan started yelling that I could beat him and to hit him again. I did and the monster recoiled even farther. There was a light shining and we could see the door to my bedroom again. Dan quickly grabbed me up and started running for my bedroom door. The Closet Monster let out a huge howl and started chasing after us. We got to my door and the Closet Monster was closing in fast behind us. He got close to us and Dan yelled, "Hit him, Sonny." I hit the monster hard with the teddy bear twice and he fell into darkness as Dan and I landed on my bed safely. The closet door shut behind us and then slowly opened up to reveal a normal closet.

A couple of months later, Mom was cooking us breakfast while Dan and I were playing finger wars. I beat Dan twice and he just laughed out loud. The Closet Monster never came back, but I keep my teddy bear near me just in case. I know one day I will conquer my fears totally and have to pass the teddy bear on to someone else, but until that time, Dan, Mom, my future baby brother, and me are happy.

The End

BIG ROBERT

They called him Big Robert. Not Robert, Big Robert. He knew there must be a law that protected him from such glaring discrimination, but for such a small company, it didn't apply to him. They made fun of him whenever the situation called for it. He was big. He weighed nearly four hundred pounds and stood six feet tall.

On this particular day, people were actually smiling at him and he didn't know why, having learned to be suspicious of anything nice that came his way on the job. Smiles and favors usually ended with a humiliation of some type, so he was leery of the bright eyes that came his way that morning, but then he saw her, a rotund woman with big hair talking to Mr. Gorman, his boss of several years. Mr. Gorman smiled at him and motioned for him to come near. He walked cautiously toward them trying to avoid looking at the huge woman standing next to Mr. Gorman. He thought everyone must think this was his joke mate and that they would endure a double humiliation at the hands of their fellow employees. They would be side-by-side joke fests.

Mr. Gorman introduced her as Sallie Mae Field. She smiled a huge smile at him and then grabbed his hand and shook it forcefully while telling him it was a mighty pleasure to meet him. She spoke with an irritating country dialect and hurt his hand when she shook it. He wanted to run away from her as quickly as possible, but Mr. Gorman kept them there by talking endlessly about his golf club collection.

When Mr. Gorman was through with his endless banter, he introduced Sallie Mae to all the employees. Everyone was happy to meet her and was thrilled with her friendly demeanor. He watched her for several days. He saw how well she interacted with the other employees. Yes, he thought, they treat you nice at first before they start calling you "Tow Truck" or "Volcano," or before they start dropping innuendos that you're so big you need to lose a half a person. He watched her.

He watched her for months and noticed the joy she brought to people whenever she was near. He noticed how she had developed camaraderie with some of the women at work. He noticed how Mr. Gorman and others had respect for Sallie Mae and wouldn't dare call her a "big fat tub of goo." He, also, noticed that he was still called "Big Robert." He noticed and he wanted to kill Sallie Mae Field.

He didn't know how he would do it. He thought about chopping her up and grinding her into chopped beef and serving her to her beloved co-workers. He thought about strangling her and sending her body to Afghanistan. He thought about stabbing her into unconsciousness and then taking her down to the sewer and letting the rats finish her off. He wanted to do all types of terrible things to her. He just had to figure out how.

He decided to follow her home one-day. She was her chipper self as she rode in her SUV on the way home. She stopped by the grocery store to get two bags of groceries. As she returned to her car, he thought to himself "*The last meal.*" He followed her home and found that he was lucky because she had a secluded driveway and garage. He decided he would come up behind her and strangle her until every breath had left her body. She got out of the car and grabbed her groceries and headed into her garage. He crept slowly behind her, reached out his arms, and then an orange fell out of her bag and she bent down to retrieve it. Caught off guard, she turned, saw Big Robert, and then smiled the brightest smile he had seen next to a star in heaven. "Hi,

Robert" she said and asked if he lived around the neighborhood. She added she was very happy to see him and asked if he wanted to have dinner with her. She said she was cooking lasagna.

Having been overwhelmed by the brightest smile this side of Yankee Stadium's lights, he accepted her invitation. He ate heartily and enjoyed her company for hours. As she walked him to her front door, she grabbed his hand and strolled. His heart was overcome and he was speechless as she opened the door. He wanted to stay. He wanted to stay forever. She kissed him on the cheek and asked him if he wanted to come back. He said yes enthusiastically. They were married a year later.

Having endured the need for respect for himself on the job, he was no longer called Big Robert, but just Robert. The employees no longer called him "Big Santa" or "Caboose Butt" either. They only called him Robert. Having found a new respect on the job, Robert moved up in position and took over Mr. Gorman's job. He and Sallie Mae had four very healthy, hefty children and lived happily for a long time.

The End

A MOTHER'S LOVE

They are driving home after having enjoyed a weekend holiday. They are in an unknown part of the country and the road is dark and woody. Her name is Katelyn Shaw; she goes by Kate and she is traveling with her son, Clay, who is asleep in the front seat. Up ahead, Kate notices something white on the road.

She pulls up behind the white object. She shines her bright lights on it and gets out and takes a look at it. She notices it is an animal of some sort, but it is strange in shape and appearance. She gets a stick and pokes it. It doesn't move. She pokes it again and it still doesn't move. Clay awakens, gets out of the car, and stops before the white animal.

"What is it?" Clay asks.

"It looks like a white bat, a huge white bat. I think its dead."

"Maybe we can take it to a vet?"

"I'm not putting that in my car."

"Maybe in the trunk?"

"The trunk has luggage. Our luggage."

Clay moves closer to the animal and touches its wings.

"Seems a shame to leave it out here-" The animal suddenly wakes up then starts to attack Clay by biting his shoulder. Clay is screaming, "GET IT OFF! GET IT OFF!" Kate screams and starts hitting at the white bat with the stick she found. She takes the stick and stabs at it until it lets go of Clay and falls to the ground. Kate quickly grabs Clay. The white thing rises, snarls at them, and then flies away. Kate lays Clay on the ground and starts tending to his wound.

"You'll be okay."

Blood is spewing quickly from the wound. Kate runs to the car and gets a towel and tears it into strips. She ties a tourniquet around Clay's shoulder to stop the bleeding. She then grabs Clay and puts him in the back seat of car. He is moaning in pain.

"I'm going to take you to a hospital. Hang on, Clay. Hang on," she says as she quickly drives down the road.

She is driving farther down the road, but there are no signs up ahead, only darkness and trees. She drives for another four miles, and still there is nothing but trees. Clay's moaning is getting worse.

"Where are we? Clay, you still with me?"

She pulls over to the side of the road. She gets out and checks on Clay. The bleeding has stopped, but Clay's eyes are now a different color and he is wheezing.

"WHAT'S HAPPENING TO YOU?" She screams.

Kate gets back in the driver's seat and starts speeding down the road. She still doesn't know where she is. Up ahead, she sees a gate with a sign that says "Sands Farm." She pulls into the gate and heads straight to the house. The house is dark, but she blows the horn loudly and continuously until she sees a light come on in the house. A man comes out and he is holding tightly to his shotgun. Kate gets out of the car and rushes to the man.

"What is it?"

"MY SON! MY SON! SOMETHING'S WRONG WITH MY SON!" Kate screams.

He lowers his gun and rushes to the back seat of the car. He looks in at Clay and turns to Kate. "Looks like he's been poisoned."

"It was some type of bat. I had never seen anything like it. Where is the nearest hospital?"

"It's three hours away."

"Mr. Sands?" Kate asks and he nods. "Is there a doctor around here?"

"We have a visiting doctor for this area, but he just care-flighted old man Wilson to the state hospital and the phones are down. Cell phones don't work too good in this area either. This is a remote area, lady. I'm sorry."

"Please, we have to do something."

"Bring him inside the barn."

They grab Clay who is moaning and groaning with each movement. They lay him on a flat table in the barn.

"He's burning up. Take off his shirt and shoes," the man says.

Kate removes his shirt, socks, and shoes and notices that Clay's feet are now webbed.

"What the hell, Oh, my God!" Cries Kate.

"What's wrong?"

"His feet! His feet are webbed together."

"He wasn't born that way?"

"NO!"

Kate goes to his hands and holds them up. "My God, they're webbing. What's happening to my son?"

"He's changing. Jesus!" The man has a pensive look.

"What do you know?"

"I've heard of strange things happening around here."

"What things?"

"There's a new facility about three miles from here. It's very secluded. 'No trespassing' signs are posted everywhere."

"What's going on there?"

"I don't know. I've just heard things."

"Like what?"

He hesitates.

"Please tell me. My son is dying."

"I've heard of strange animals, weird experiments, and people disappearing. People are moving away from this area in droves."

"I have to go there."

"It might be dangerous."

"My son is changing. They must know something about this. I have to go there. What's that noise?"

They look toward the window and see the white bat trying to get inside the barn. Kate screams. The white bat is pounding at the window.

"Stop it!" Kate screams as Sands rushes to the window with a pitchfork and jabs at the white thing. The bat lets out a loud screech and flies away. Sands quickly closes the window and puts a piece of furniture in front of it.

"What does it want?"

"I think it wants your son."

Clay lets out a loud scream and Kate runs to him. She grabs his hands, but they are completely webbed together. "My God look at his hands."

"He's changing into one of those bats," Mr. Sands responds. "It wants him. That thing outside wants him."

"Where is the facility you're talking about?"

"You can't go out with that thing out there.

"I know. It's gotten bigger."

"What?"

"It's gotten bigger. I've got to get my son some help. I've got to! Will you protect my son while I go to that facility?"

"Lady, I have a wife and kids."

"Please, I beg you."

"I'll do what I can, but hurry back. I don't know what I'm up against. That thing is out there."

"I'm going to run to the car. Hopefully it's gone away. You have your shotgun?"

"Yes."

"Shoot that mother if it comes out."

Mr. Sands goes to his toolbox in the corner and gets a pistol out of it. "Here's a pistol. Take the main road to West View. Turn left. You'll hit a trail. From there you're on your own. Be careful."

Kate grabs the pistol and her keys and heads toward the door. She holds the door ajar and turns back to say something when the white bat thing tries to come into the barn. Kate screams for help and starts pushing at the door. Sands runs to the door and helps push the door closed then locks it.

"It's gotten bigger and stronger," Kate says.

"You can't go out there," Sands insists.

"I have to. I have to for my son. Get the shotgun."

He gets the shotgun and Kate cocks her pistol. "Ready," says Kate.

He nods and she opens the door slowly then runs out. She hears the white thing fly over and shoots at it. Sands fires the shotgun at it. Kate rushes to the car, starts it, and drives off. Sands closes the barn door and puts a plank across it. He hears the car drive away and the white thing flying over. It flies into the door repeatedly. He holds his shotgun close until the thumping at the door stops.

Clay starts screaming and thrashing about. Sands gets some straps and ties Clay down. Clay lies still and starts to moan. Sands, now curious, gets closer to Clay and lifts his upper lips. He sees that Clay's teeth have changed to fangs. Clay snaps at Sands, who quickly moves his hands away. He sits down close to Clay and holds his shotgun near while watching the barn door and the window.

"My God, it's gotten bigger." Kate says driving into the night. The road is dark. She's been driving for 15 minutes. There is nothing but darkness and trees. Then Kate sees a road that leads to a trail. She follows the trail and it gets denser and denser until there is nothing but grass. She keeps going until she picks up another trail that eventually leads to a fence. She parks her car near the fence, gets out, and starts walking. She throws a stick at the fence to see if it has an electric current. It does not. She touches the fence, grabs hold of it and climbs it. She starts to hear strange noises as she walks beside the fence until she sees a light up ahead. As she gets closer, she sees it is a security post. A single security guard mans it. He is watching TV and not paying attention to the outside. Kate crouches low and starts to crawl toward the post. She gets closer and stops on the side of the guardhouse. She crawls to the area where the light is not shining and crawls slowly toward the tall white building ahead avoiding any lighted patches. She crawls toward a side door and checks to see if it is unlocked. Someone is coming, so she ducks behind a bush. The person comes out of the side door and walks toward the front. Kate instantly reaches her hand out to put a wedge in the door then sneaks into the building. She dodges around corners while avoiding people and finally comes to a hall where there are eerie sounds coming from behind each door. She looks into the window of one door and nearly screams in horror. She stops, slides down to the floor, and whimpers while saying her son's name. She hears someone coming, wipes her tears, and dodges around another corner. The person starts to get closer and she goes into an open room. The lights automatically come on as she enters. She tries to get out of the room, but the door shuts and locks. She hears someone talking in the next room and decides to follow the voice. She comes to an office, enters it, and the chair at the desk turns around. A man is sitting there.

"Hello, Mrs. Smith," he says.

"How do you know my name?"

"We know all about you. You taught school for 12 years and then you opened a bakery shop. You have 3 children-"

"WHAT'S HAPPENING TO MY SON?"

"He's changing. He's becoming one of them, but we can stop it, Mrs. Smith."

"How?"

"We have an antidote that you must give him before the transformation," he says

"Give it to me, please."

"On one condition. You must never go to the authorities on us."

"Why shouldn't I?"

"Because you don't know who we work for, Mrs. Smith, and I wouldn't want anything to happen to you or your family. Here, Mrs. Smith, go quickly. You don't have much time," he says and gives her the syringe.

Kate rushes out of the building and runs to her car. She forgets to tell him about the white bat, but assumes he already knows. She knows she must get to her son immediately and rushes down the road into darkness. She has an eerie feeling she is being followed, but doesn't look back. She drives up to the farm and heads straight to the barn. She blows her horn so that Sands knows she is coming. He opens the door and motions for her to hurry inside while looking up at the sky. She runs in with the syringe. Sands is about to bolt the door when the white bat bursts through and flies in. The bat has grown to the size of a human. It quickly flies toward Kate and knocks her down, sending the syringe forward into a stack of hay. Clay lets out a screechy scream. Kate notices he now resembles more closely a bat and rushes to find the syringe in the stack of hay. The white bat flies at her, but Sands fires a shot at it.

The white bat flies toward Sands before he can reload his shotgun and knocks him unconscious against the wall. It then lands and turns slowly toward Kate. Kate finds the syringe then rushes to Clay and stabs him with it. Clay and the white bat both let out a loud screech that shatters all the windows of the barn, house, and cars. The white bat then heads toward Kate and Clay. She screams, goes to a bale of hay and retrieves a pitchfork. She points it at the white bat, ready to do battle.

"STAY AWAY FROM MY SON!"

Just then a net is thrown over the white bat and it struggles to get free, but the men in uniform shoot it with a sedative. It falls to the ground and they grab it and rush it into a medical truck. They speed off. Kate goes to her son who is slowly turning back to full human form. She hears Sands moan and goes to him and helps him up.

"My windows!" He says groggily.

"I know," Kate says while helping him walk.

"How's your son?"

"He's changing back."

"You know, I think it's time to move."

The next morning, Kate and Sands put Clay in the car and lies him down in the back seat. They have cleared all the glass from the car and the car still starts.

"He's still weak," says Kate.

"He'll be okay. Stick to the main road and turn left at the stop sign. That'll take you to 121, which will head you into the city. Don't expect rain, so you'll be fine."

"Thank you for your help."

"You're welcome."

"What are you going to do?" Kate asks.

"I think I'm going to get out of here as soon as possible. It's becoming a remote area and I see why. Are you going to the authorities?"

"I don't know. That man at the facility made a comment, "You don't know who we're working for.""

"And you don't. I'm keeping my mouth shut. Maybe you should do the same."

"Yes, maybe," Kate says and gets in her car, waves to Sands, and drives off.

While driving she passes a small town. There is a police station nearby. She stops and goes inside. Everyone stops and stares at her. An eerie feeling creeps up her spine and the words "You don't know who we work for" sound in her ears.

"Does anyone know where Highway 39 is?" Kate asks.

"It's down the road to the left," someone says.

"Thank you."

Kate goes out the door, heads to her car, and drives away quickly, never looking back.

The End

THE BOOK OF KINGS

And as the king of Israel was passing by upon the wall, there cried a woman unto him, saying, Help, my lord, O king.

And he said, If the Lord do not help thee, whence shall I help thee? out of the barnfloor, or out of the winepress?

And the king said unto her, What aileth thee? And she answered, This woman said unto me, Give thy son, that we may eat him today, and we will eat my son tomorrow.

So we boiled my son, and did eat him: and I said unto her on the next day, Give thy son, that we may eat him: and she hath hid her son.

2 Kings 6:26-29
-Holy Bible (King James Version)

Verona was hungry. In fact, the whole country was hungry. Everyone was in the mist of a famine. The rains had not come for two years and crops, plants, and animals had died. Verona sat on the porch and smoked her Benson & Hedges and wondered what she was going to feed herself and her son tonight. She would smoke and sometimes talk out of the side of her mouth with her lips pooched out and her body in a haughty stance that reflected, "Don't mess with me or I'll kick your ass" mode. She hated the fact that she smoked, but it curbed her appetite and she needed that right now. She sat on her porch and watched the neighborhood play, and then she saw Little Daryl walk by. *"Damn, that's a hefty boy. I could eat off of him for thirty days,"* she thought to herself and then an idea came to her.

Little Daryl Jacob was the only son of an older couple who lived next door to Verona. They had had Daryl late in life and not having the patience to raise a young child, usually indulged Daryl with everything his heart desired. In his case, that meant food, so Little Daryl was morbidly obese. Verona watched Daryl go down the street to play. She watched his arms jiggle and thought about fatback for her greens. She watched his thighs waddle and thought about ham hocks for her red beans. Yes, she had an idea. All she had to do was come correct and put her most smoothest *Mack* on.

Verona knocked on Mr. and Mrs. Jacob's door and put forth her brightest smile. They welcomed her hesitantly and invited her to sit in their living room. Verona was considered the loudmouth of the neighborhood and showed little decorum.

"What can we do for you, Verona?" Mrs. Jacob asked.

"Mr. and Mrs. Jacob, there's a famine going through the land and everyone's hungry. Wouldn't you agree?"

"Oh yes, we're hungry too, and we don't have any food to spare," Mr. Jacob replied aggressively.

"I propose a plan that may help us to satisfy our hunger and help us to live longer."

"What is that, Verona?" Mrs. Jacob asked.

"We eat our sons."

"What?" Mr. Jacob said.

"We eat our sons. We eat your son, and then we eat my son. Let's face it, your son is juicy."

"But your son is muscular, well-built, and good-looking."

"He fine. He fine."

"He doesn't have a lot of meat on him."

"What we can do is soak him in a tub with some meat tenderizer for a couple days, cook him, and he'll be succulent. Just succulent!"

So the Jacobs agreed to cook their son, but Verona couldn't just sit back quietly. She organized a big neighborhood barbecue of Little Daryl. Everybody in the neighborhood came to the barbecue. They hired the best DJ and Mr. Jenkins, the best cook, to do the cooking and everyone brought their favorite dishes to share. Verona was up dancing when the DJ put on Morris Day and the Time's "Jungle Love."

"HEY, THAT'S MY JAM!" Verona exclaimed while swinging her hips.

Someone yelled, "Who wants to play some Spades?!" And someone else said "I got the dominoes!"

Verona flirtingly went to Mr. Jenkins and said, "Mr. Jenkins, those are the best ribs. They taste better than that one rib they give you at Medieval Times. It's one rib, but it's the best rib in the world and yours comes close. Real close. Now, give me some of that seasoning salt for my sandwich."

Someone put on Kool and the Gang's "Celebration" and Verona yelled, "HEY, THAT'S MY JAM!"

Yes, everyone was having a grand ole time in the Jacobs' backyard. Books were gathered and dominoes were slamming. There was plenty of food and good music. You could hear different pieces of conversation throughout the backyard. In one part of the yard:

"Yeah, my baby mama threw me out and then my other baby mama threw me out. They say I don't want to work. How can I work? I'm weak. I ain't had nothing to eat in two days. Let me get you a plate of food."

"Just get me two fingers. I'm on a diet."

"Girl, the whole land's on a diet."

"In that case, get me some thigh."

In another part of the yard:

"Girl, he so fine. Wouldn't his name look good on my arm with the Leprechaun tattoo?"

And in another part of the yard:

"GIVE ME TWENTY-FIVE!"

"Oooh, you reneged. Give me two books." responded another player

The Jacobs called Verona into the kitchen.

"Verona, where's your son? We bought a tub full of meat tenderizer with the insurance money from Little Daryl."

"Oh, I'll get him."

Verona rushed out to her son, Tyrell. Tyrell was talking to some girl, trying to get his score on.

"Tyrell, I need to talk to you."

"Not now, Mama. I'll talk with you later."

"Tyrell-"

"Mama!"

Verona grabbed Tyrell by the ear and drug him over to the fence.

"Boy, when I'm talking to you, you better listen."

"Dawg, Mama. What?"

"They ready to make hotdogs out of you. Here, you take this airplane ticket and go stay with Big Mama. And remember, if Big Mama croak, find her stash before Cousin Tooky 'nem get to it."

"Okay, Mama. I love you."

"Love you too. Now git!"

Verona started dancing again, but then Mr. and Mrs. Jacob called her back into the kitchen.

"Where's your son, Verona?"

"Oh, he went to Vegas to get him some before we cook him, but he's coming back. Don't worry."

"But-"

"Don't worry. He's just gone to get him a little something-something. Didn't Little Daryl get him some before you cooked him?"

"No. He was a virgin."

"Oh, that's too bad. But you know my son's going to be succulent. Just succulent! Well now, I'm gonna grab me some barbecued buttocks." Verona said.

Someone put on Rick James' "Super Freak" while she was going out the patio door. "HEY, THAT'S MY JAM!" Verona yelled while dancing her way to the middle of the backyard.

Mr. and Mrs. Jacob watched Verona as she danced and had fun. She had grabbed a cooked arm and was dancing with it. They felt like fools. To make amends, they took Little Daryl's head and put it in a cake cover on top of the refrigerator. They would bury it in the morning.

When they woke up in the morning, they retrieved Little Daryl's head from atop the refrigerator. They noticed that some-one had sliced his ears off, but they took the head to a gravesite and buried it anyway. They stayed for a little while, but then got hungry and went home and ate what was left of Little Daryl. It was enough for one day and the next and the next and the next...

The End

PARTNERS

They roamed together. They hunted, played, and loved together. They were inseparable.

She could hear the drums beating. It was loud in her head like standing on a sidewalk in a parade as the marching band went by. The closer the airplane got to the jungle, the louder the drums beat in her mind. She knew it was a warning, but she could not tell her husband. He would not listen.

She was Alexi Carmichael, a young, rich widow who had had the luck to marry Roan Carmichael, an adventurer and hunter. Luck, only by other women's standards, because Roan was dashing, handsome, and famous or, rather, infamous for his escapades throughout the world. He had hunted some of the biggest and most nearly extinct animals in the world, and while he was the darling of the jet-set crowd, animal activists around the globe despised him.

Roan never cared for the jet set and only had disdain for the animal protesters. They all simply got in the way of his next conquest. He lived and cared only for the adventure, that is, until he met Alexi who captured his heart the minute he laid eyes on her. He knew it was a mistake to bring her into his lifestyle, but he could not live without her. She had traveled with him for the past two years but lately she had been bemoaning their lifestyle. She wanted a family and to settle down. The very thought of not being able to live the lifestyle he had accustomed himself to was demeaning in his eyes, yet he loved and adored Alexi and would do anything for her. He just never wanted to end up hating her in the end for changing him into something he was not. His greatest fear was of losing Alexi and it was a fear that was growing stronger by the day. He would have to make a choice soon and both decisions had a very sad outcome.

This was the last one, Alexi told herself. She could go no further with Roan. The allure of different continents and people of strange cultures and religions had worn thin in her eyes. She wanted a simple life of bacon and eggs and crying children. She would return home after this trip with or without Roan, except the distant drumming had a different story. It told a story of forbidding nuances, of strange magic and alluring potions, of exotic movements and restless mysticisms. It told a story of death, a story of her death.

The plane would be landing soon. Of course, there would be people with exotic clothing and animals in straw cages waiting restlessly at the airport. She was used to it by now. She had hoped they would stay in the town area, but Roan had a house in the middle of the jungle, of course. As the plane landed, the beating seemed to subside a little. Maybe it was giving her a chance to convince Roan to leave the jungle, or maybe it was the calm before the storm, whichever, she was grateful for the moment of peace.

At the airport Rumsfed, an old friend of Roan who occasionally hunted with him, met them. Alexi despised him. He was loud, crass, and an obnoxious flirt who drank all the time and chased the local women. He picked up Roan, put him over his shoulder, and twirled him around then gave her a sloppy kiss on the neck.

"Are you a sight for sore eyes?" Rumsfed said while slapping Roan on the shoulder.

"You old stud. They haven't put you out of your misery yet?" Roan laughed.

"Not yet. Alexi! Beautiful as always."

"Thank you, Rumsfed," she said giving him a wry smile.

"Come. Let's go to the house," Rumsfed said as they followed him away from the busy airport.

As they drove through the jungle in a jeep with no cover on top, there seem to be hidden shadows around every corner. The shadows cast darker shades that seemed longer and odd in shape, making the jungle appear haunted and foreboding. Limbs on trees hung longer than usual, trying to reach and touch them as they passed by. Roan and Rumsfed laughed and told jokes, not noticing the thickness of the air around them, but Alexi sensed it and she wanted to scream.

As they reached the house, Suni, an old native friend, was waiting on the porch. He had a look of concern on his face, but Roan and Rumsfed did not notice. They only emerged from the jeep, grabbed their old friend, and danced a dance of celebration to see him. He was a little reserved with Alexi and Roan took notice, but Rumsfed grabbed them all in a bear hug and rushed them into the house for food and drinks. Servants came out and grabbed their luggage while they entered the house. They immediately went into the den and Rumsfed started pouring drinks for everyone. Alexi excused herself to her room while they told stories of jollies and conquests.

The house was surprisingly beautiful to Alexi. She entered their bedroom, which had lavish paintings and a draped canopy bed. The drum beating had come back. There were exotic pieces everywhere and they seemed to loom at her as she lay across the bed. She wanted to be far, far away from here, but Alexi closed her eyes and tried to sleep.

It was dark and the men gathered on the porch to watch the stars and listen for sounds from the jungle. The alcohol had put them all in a calm stupor and they were relaxed and calm. All problems seemed distant for now, especially for Roan. Rumsfed excused himself to the gentlemen's room and Roan and Suni were left alone. A look of concern immediately came to Suni's face.

"What is it, Suni?" Roan asked.

"Your quest is for the white lions. Is it not?"

"It is."

"Roan, the locals believe they possess magic. There has been a lot of stirring among the natives. I do not wish harm to you. Nor to Alexi-"

"I'm not afraid of a bunch of natives. We're pretty protected here," said Roan.

"You are surrounded by natives. Your servants are natives."

"I'll get extra men from the town."

"Roan, you are a good friend of mine. Chase the elephant, the rhinoceros, or the zebra. Do not hunt the white lions. The karma around you and Alexi is not good-"

Just then, they heard Alexi scream. Everyone rushed to Alexi's room. Roan rushed to Alexi while she pointed at the window. Suni, Rumsfed, and other servants went out through Alexi's window searching for an intruder. Roan comforted Alexi in his arms.

"What did you see?" Roan asked.

"It was a native dressed like a witch doctor," Alexi said.

"Are you sure?"

"Yes, I'm sure," Alexi said now irritated.

Suni and Rumsfed returned.

"We saw nothing," Rumsfed said. "Are you sure you weren't dreaming?"

"I'm sure," Alexi said.

"Roan," Suni stated with a warning in his voice.

"Not now, Suni," Roan replied.

"What's, not now?" Alexi asked alarmed.

"It's nothing. Try to get some sleep. I'll have guards posted outside your window," Roan said.

They all were leaving Alexi's room, but before they left, Rumsfed noticed a little voodoo doll and put it in his pocket. Suni excused himself and left the residence. Rumsfed and Roan returned to the den for more drinks. Rumsfed had a look of concern on his face.

"What were you and Suni talking about?" Rumsfed asked.

"He said the natives were restless about our hunt for the white lion."

"Roan, Alexi's-"

"I know."

"Why don't you return home and take time to decide. It could do you both some good."

"I think I've already decided," Roan said.

Rumsfed stared at his friend. He wanted to tell him of his lonely life and lonely nights, but decided against it. "I've had enough to drink. I'm going to bed." Rumsfed said as he left the room.

Roan was left alone in the den. He had another drink before returning to Alexi. He sat on the bed and watched her sleep. She stirred restlessly under the sheets and blanket. Roan took off his clothes and got into bed with her. He caressed her body and she stared awake sleepily. He grabbed her and started making love to her. Alexi begged with her body for Roan to choose her, but Roan made love just to let go. They both lay sleeping in each other's arms until the next morning.

Roan and Rumsfed left for the hunt the next morning before Alexi was awake. They traveled a good distance from the house into the depth of the jungle. Roan was feeling more preoccupied with every step he took. Rumsfed noticed his friend's lack of concentration and wanted to say something to him, but traveled on within the jungle with him.

Alexi woke with the beating of the drum pounding in her head. She was alone in the room. She got up then bathed and dressed in a hurry. She knew guards were posted outside her window, but a feeling of uneasiness would not leave her. She was about to put on her jacket when she saw him. He was covered in white and red paint with wild straw hair coming from his head. His teeth were sharpened and stained with black rot. She could not scream for the terror. He came toward her and backed her into the wall. She was about to scream when he put a necklace around her head.

"For protection," he growled at her and quickly left her room.

Alexi looked at the strange necklace decorated with bones and stones. She knew what she must do. She had to fight for Roan. She had to find him and convince him to come with her. She ran into the jungle looking for him.

Rumsfed could go no farther, but Roan was driven. They walked deeper into the jungle and started canvassing the area. Exhausted, Rumsfed turned to his old friend.

"I guess I'm out of practice," Rumsfed said.

"You old horse! You're never out of practice."

Rumsfed leaned up against a tree breathing rapidly. "You know, Roan, at my age a nice home with children and a wife to love doesn't sound so bad. I've done this for far too long."

"You're just tired. We'll take a break here," Roan said.

"Yes, Roan, I'm tired. How many animals can you kill to satisfy your hunger for the hunt? There are too many, but who can satisfy your hunger for love? I've seen how you look at Alexi. To lose such a love would be a soulful loss. Go to her, Roan."

"I can't change who I am, Rumsfed."

Just then, Rumsfed produced the voodoo doll from his pocket.

"What's that?" Roan asked.

"I found it in Alexi's room last night when-"

And then they heard a roar from up ahead. Roan positioned his gun and walked slowly toward the sound.

"Roan, no!" Rumsfed, from behind, called ahead out-of-breath.

Roan's heart was beating fast. This was the thrill he lived for. This was his life. He walked slowly toward the roar. He saw it. It was beautiful, white, almost illuminating. It was lying up ahead and seemed to notice Roan, but kept still. Roan raised his gun and fired. Just then, Rumsfed came running from behind. He screamed at Roan to look behind him. Roan turned and came face to face with another huge white lion. It stared in Roan's eyes for a brief second. Its massive face was so close to Roan's that he could feel its breath, and then it disappeared right before his eyes. Roan could hear the drums beating now.

Alexi searched the jungle even though she was frightened. The beating started getting louder, crushing her ears. She turned and ran back to the house. She put her hands over her ears and, in doing so, a branch snatched the protective necklace up from her throat and the beating stopped. The silence was even more deafening than the beating. She slowly ascended the stairs to the house. There were no servants around. She walked into their room and shut the door. The room seemed larger than usual in her eyes. She walked slowly toward the bed. She turned, and then it leaped upon her.

Roan could hear the drum beating and immediately thought of Alexi. He ran toward the house, leaving Rumsfed to follow, breathless, behind him. Rumsfed could not keep up and stopped near a tree to catch his breath, but Roan was running like a wild animal toward his house. He had to get to Alexi quickly or it would be too late. The drums were pounding in his ears when he came to the house, but they stopped as soon as he opened the door. He noticed the silence and called for Alexi. He walked slowly toward their bedroom. He opened the door and saw the blood. A single tear came from his eye before it leaped upon him.

They roamed together. They hunted, played, and loved together. They were inseparable.

The End

CLOTHES MAKE THE MAN

My washing machine was on the fritz. Again. My name is Mary West and I just wanted to wash a few clothes for the week and a couple of things for the school reunion picnic. I especially wanted to wash the lingerie Allen had given me before he died. It had been a year and a half since his death and I thought it was time to, well, not to move on, but to start anew. I should have washed them by hand on my own, but I just wasn't thinking. I was excited once again about meeting someone, yet I was scared too. So I brought my little bag of laundry to Polly's Laundry Mat. No one was around. It was a bright sunny day and the sunshine inside the laundromat made everything glow and shine. I thought I might be in Heaven inside a place lined with the Streets of Gold. I started the three washing machines. The first machine was for my bright colors and the second my dark colors. The third was for fine washables and that machine only had a few pieces in it: a couple of bras and camisoles and the delicate bra and panty set Allen had bought for me before he went away.

I remember when he brought them home. It was not a special occasion or holiday. It was something he did out of the blue. And they were blue, royal blue, and they had my initials on them. I was so outdone. They were beautiful. He asked me to put them on and I did. I came out of the bathroom feeling a little shy with them on and he just watched me. He then came to me and gently removed the bra and the panties; he lifted me up; he carried me to bed and made love to me for hours. It was the most romantic thing he had ever given me, not just the lingerie, but also the lovemaking. He totally gave to me for hours and asked nothing in return. He only wanted to make me happy and he did. Whenever we argued or experienced a rough patch, I would always think of that moment of love he showed toward me. It was etched in my heart forever.

The clothes were on the spin cycle when I decided to go to my car and get a magazine to read. I guess I took a little longer than I should have because when I returned to the machines there were two girls stealing from my washers. I ran to them.

"Hey, what are you doing? That's my machine," I cried.

One of the girls had Allen's lingerie in her hand.

"Give it back," I yelled.

I tried wrestling them away from her. One of them pulled a knife and stabbed me.

Darkness.

***

Mrs. Edward Pearson Rockwood III was totally broke. Her successful husband had made some very bad investment choices before he died and left her with a huge estate tax and other debts she had little or no knowledge as to how to pay back. She roughly only had minor assets, which she was slowly selling off one by one. She had no one to help her except for a faithful yet notorious butler, Mr. Raynard, who was waiting to get an expensive piece of jewelry or artwork for lack of pay and his pain and suffering. Mrs. Rockwood had no one to turn to, having ignored her family for years, and was only barely tolerated by the upper crust in local society because of her husband. She was considered gaudy, loud, and crude, especially in her attire. She dressed for attention, the upper crust would all say, and that made the men stare and the women angry.

Mrs. Rockwood was upset more than usual today. She had

just received an invitation for dinner from a John Folders who was a fat little balding man with a wealthy empire of his own. *He could buy gaudy*, she thought to herself, but first she needed the right outfit to wear. She called for Raynard. As she called for him she was diligently looking through closets and drawers searching for the right outfit. Clothes were strewn everywhere. It was a mixture of dirty and clean clothes together.

"RAYNARD, RAYNARD!" She yelled. "Where is my pink Chanel suit?"

"It's in your hamper, Madam," said Raynard as he appeared in her room.

"It's dirty? Why isn't it at the cleaners?"

"You haven't paid your bill, Madam."

"Damn! Maybe I can wash it in the washing machine?"

"You sold the washing machine, Madam."

"I did not."

"Yes, Madam, you did."

"Well hell, how am I going to have this date? I can't go looking like a rag doll." Mrs. Rockwood started hitting at flies with a fly swatter she got off her dresser. She left the window open instead of running the air conditioner to keep her electric bill low.

"By the way, Madam, when are you going to pay me? All the other staff have left."

"I DON'T KNOW, RAYNARD!"

"Perhaps you can give me this Ming Vase," he said while greedily rubbing the vase on her nightstand.

Mrs. Rockwood quickly swatted his hands away from her vase with her fly swatter.

"Not on your life, Butler Boy."

***

I woke up and Mom was sitting by my bed crying in the

Emergency Room. I had an agonizing pain in my stomach. I tried to rise up. Mom started yelling for the doctor. The doctor came rushing over.

"Whoa, Ma'am," he said while gently pressing me down. "You've had a nasty cut."

"Where am I?" I said groggily.

"You're in the hospital, Honey," Mom said sniffing.

"You've been stabbed, Mrs. West. You can go home in an hour or two as long as you take it easy for about a week. I'll be back," the doctor said walking away.

"Stabbed? Stabbed? Oh, I remember. Allen's lingerie! AL-LEN'S LINGERIE!" I screamed while trying to get out of bed.

"No, Mary. You have to be still, Honey, or you'll bust your stitches," she said trying to hold me down and keep me down.

"NO!! Allen's lingerie! I have to get them."

"DOCTOR! DOCTOR! HURRY!!" Mom screamed.

The doctor rushed over with a shot of tranquilizer and gave it to me quickly. I began to settle down and then felt drowsy.

"Allen's lingerie," I whispered as I fell into a deep sleep.

***

Mrs. Rockwood was diligently searching through a stack of dirty clothes to find what she needed to wear. She finally came across a pink sheer blouse that she thought would be perfect for her date. Raynard was busy dusting and admiring her Ming Vase.

"Okay Raynard, I need you to wash out my clothes and hang them up for me."

"I don't wash clothes, Madam."

"THEN WHAT DO YOU DO, RAYNARD?!"

"I'm a butler, Madam. I buttle."

"You know, Raynard. You can-"

"May I remind you again, Madam that I am the only ser-vant you have left?"

"THEN WHY DON'T YOU SERVE?!"

"I do, Madam, but I don't wash. Would you like some tea?" He said while leaving the room. Mrs. Rockwood threw a shoe at him and missed.

"Oh, I'll go wash them myself. I still remember how, I think," she said while grabbing a handful of clothes.

***

I had to get them back. I had to. My mom took a nap and I snuck out of her house. I went back to Polly's Laundry Mat to look for those girls. I didn't know what I would do when I found them. I guess I'd beg for my lingerie back. I walked into Polly's and there was an old man sweeping. He looked shocked when he saw me.

"You're as pale as a ghost. You need to be in bed," he said.

"I was robbed here today. They stabbed me and took some-thing very valuable to me."

"Was it jewelry?"

"No," I started to cry. "It was some lingerie my late husband gave me. They mean a lot to me. Please, can you help me?"

"I dunno, Ma'am. What did the people look like?" He asked.

"One had on a blue bandana-"

"Oh! Look Miss, forget about your clothes and go home. You don't want to mess with those girls. They're Clothes Gyp-sies; they steal people's clothes out the washer when they leave them."

"Where can I find them?"

"Miss, those girls can be dangerous. Go home. You have your life and your memories."

"I DON'T WANT MY MEMORIES. I WANT ALLEN'S LINGERIE!" I yelled then began to feel faint.

The old man grabbed me and sat me down on a bench near the door. He used a paper towel to wipe the sweat from my brow. "Listen-"

"Please, I beg you. They mean the world to me. The world." I said, barely breathing.

***

The sun was shining, but this part of town seemed darker than usual. I walked for several blocks passing old cars, condemned buildings, and trash tumbleweeds, and then I saw them, a group of people in an alley wearing all types of clothing from new to old to fashionable to torn. There were bundles of clothes in the corner of the alleyway. They seemed to be chanting a song. When I approached they all quickly gathered weapons in their hands. The one who must have been the leader signaled them to put down their weapons and then she walked up to me.

"What do you want?" She said.

"Two of your members stabbed me and took my clothes."

"You're lucky they didn't kill you. What do you want?"

"There was a bra and panty set-"

"And?"

"I need them back. They mean a great deal to me. My late husband gave them to me. Please, can I have them back?"

"Who stabbed you?" She asked.

I looked around at all the weirdly dressed people and recognized the two girls who attacked me. I pointed them out.

"Give 'em back, now," the leader commanded.

The one who stabbed me got behind a car and took my lingerie off then threw them at my feet. The panties were soiled in between the crotch. A fury rose up inside me that I had never felt before. I started toward her but the leader stopped me with a stick.

"You have your clothes. Now leave before you get hurt."

"Sorry. It's that time of the month," the one who had worn my underwear said.

Then she started to laugh. The fury inside me rose even higher and I went toward her. Darkness.

***

What happened next was a blur to me. I remember being knocked to the ground and someone saying, "Let's go to Polly's." Someone grabbed me from the ground and put all types of clothing on me. I was bleeding from my stitches and blood was soaking through my clothes.

I seem to remember being sat down on the floor near a washer. Everyone started singing and clapping and then a gaudily dressed woman pulled up in an expensive car, got out, and came inside. Everyone got quiet and scattered. The woman came in angry and was very preoccupied, talking to herself while putting clothes in a washer. Then one of the Gypsies came up behind her and scared her.

"Hello, my dear lady," the Gypsy said.

"What do you want?" She gasped.

Another Gypsy came from the other side and grabbed her clothes. The woman tried to run, but other Gypsies soon surrounded her. They encircled her and started pushing her back and forth. She screamed and tried to escape, but they just kept pushing her toward the center of the circle. Someone said, "Play a song." And they all started singing. They lifted me up and put me in the circle with this woman then motioned for me to dance. I started dancing deliriously while this other woman was hysterical and trying to get away. They sang:

"Clothes make the man. Oh, clothes make the man."
"You can't be Ivana without the right clothes."
"You can't be Diana without the right clothes."
"Clothes make the man. Oh, clothes make the man."

They repeated this several times. Then they stabbed the woman and left us both in the laundry mat sitting by some washers bleeding and unconscious with Allen's lingerie at my side.

The End

I MURDERED A SNOWMAN

It smiled at me. Every time I went to the window, his motherfucking ass was smiling at me. I wanted to shoot his white face off this Earth for good. The motherfucker was too happy. He even had his hand up in a constant wave position.

"Say Hi, Motherfucker! Just say Hi."

The son of a bitch was fat too. I wanted to run his fat ass around the block a hundred times. I could just pinch his fat and twist and twist. I had to get ready for work and pulled the shades closed, but I knew he was smiling at me through the blinds. It made me sick. I got dressed and walked out to my car. I gave the big fat motherfucker a snarl and drove off.

***

Mr. Kithara valued his Christmas decoration with a warm heart. Every year he prided himself on his home décor despite the weather—and it was warm. Los Angeles was particularly warm this Christmas and it didn't feel like Christmas. It usually didn't, but Mr. Kithara didn't care. He wanted a decorated house and he spent a great deal of money on it. He had both white and colored Christmas lights. He decorated his windows with Christmas posters and ornaments and even decorated his bushes. He also decorated his yard with pop-up Christmas lights around the trimmings. It didn't matter to him that no other house on the street was decorated; he wanted to celebrate Christmas in high fashion. Feeling this way, Mr. Kithara had one vice: his inflatable snowman. He prided himself on the huge snowman that adorned his front yard every Christmas. He took joy in the snowman's jolliness and happy demeanor. Mr. Kithara tied his favorite tie around the snowman's neck to show the snowman that he loved him. When Mr. Kithara was feeling sad, he would go outside and talk to his happy friend, which he had christened "Mr. Snowman."

Mrs. Kithara thought her husband foolish, foolish for spending so much money on Christmas, foolish for decorating the house, and most certainly foolish for relishing a stupid snowman. They were from China and didn't celebrate Christmas over there. Maybe in recent years they adopted the culture, but most of their lives they never celebrated Christmas. She thought the holiday was a waste of money and materials. She could halfway tolerate the holiday if it wasn't for her husband's bizarre behavior and his obsession with the snowman.

Mr. Kithara awoke one morning and went outside to say hello to his snowman, only to find Mr. Snowman flat and deflated to the ground. He was both angry and confused until he got a little closer and saw that Mr. Snowman had been stabbed. He let out a howl then ran into the house and called the police. Mrs. Kithara ran downstairs to see what all the commotion was about.

"Good riddance," Mrs. Kithara said about the snowman, then smirked and went back upstairs. Mr. Kithara was very upset though. He called the police begging them to do something; they only said they would send someone out to take a report. Mr. Kithara was visibly disappointed, feeling that they should have sent a SWAT team out to investigate and kill the suspected murderer that took the life of Mr. Snowman. He went out into the front yard and picked up Mr. Snowman then buried him in the back yard while vowing revenge. Mr. Kithara immediately went to the store and bought another snowman, but this one was bigger. Mrs. Kithara could only put her hands on her hips in dismay as Mr. Kithara put up the giant snowman. He christened this one "Mr. Snowman II" and set little mousetraps around the snowman just in case anyone should try to kill him. "This should do it," Mr. Kithara said to himself and returned to his house satisfied.

***

I drove home only to find the motherfucker had gotten bigger. *Did the fucker take steroids? Big ole bitch!* I wanted to kick his ass. And what kind of neighbor was this that aggravated me with this fucking monstrosity?

"I'll get you. I'll get you for laughing at me. Big show boat-ass motherfucker," I muttered to myself as I went inside the house and pulled all the shades down.

***

Mr. Kithara woke up happy. He was going to say good morning to Mr. Snowman II. He put on his slippers and went outside only to find all the mousetraps set and Mr. Snowman II lying flat on the front lawn. He, too, had been stabbed. Mr. Kithara wanted to cry as he bent down and cradled Mr. Snowman II.

"REVENGE! REVENGE! REVENGE!" He screamed as Mrs. Kithara looked at her husband and shook her head.

Mr. Kithara then got up, buried Mr. Snowman II, and went back to the store and got another snowman. This time he filled the snowman with helium. Whoever would dare stab this snowman, which he christened "Ed", was in for a big surprise.

***

She wanted to go out with friends. She was actually in a good mood until she saw him. He made her blood boil. She wanted to shoot him with an AK-47, but her cousin wouldn't loan it to her. So she waited by her car looking the other way from him. Her friends pulled up and then she felt better. She got in their car and drove off.

They pulled up in front of her house about three o'clock in the morning. They were all loud and inebriated. She got out of the car and staggered.

She started yelling. "Big fat motherfucker! I'll kill you! You son of a bitch! Someone give me a knife. Give me a knife," she said swaying back and forth.

"Kill him! Kill that big motherfucker," one of her girl-friends yelled.

"I've got my butcher knife I keep under the seat," another girlfriend said.

"Give it to me. I'm gonna cut you. Cut you," she said while her girlfriend gave her the butcher knife.

She ran across the street while her girlfriends urged her on. She yelled that famous Flintstone's expletive "Hakidocki!" then went up to the snowman and stabbed him. He exploded, sending her up into a tree, then she fell to the ground semiconscious. She could somewhat hear her girlfriends' car tires squeal then speed-ily drive off. She could barely feel herself being dragged into a house before she lost consciousness completely.

She woke up tied to a chair. A Chinese man dressed in an-cient Chinese warrior gear held a gleaming sword in his hands. She began to cry loudly.

"DON'T KILL ME! PLEASE! DON'T KILL ME!" She cried.

"You murdered my snowmen. You gonna pay," Mr. Kithara said while swinging his sword back and forth then taking a war-rior's stance.

Mrs. Kithara came down to the basement and protested loudly to her husband in Chinese.

"She killed my snowmen. She gonna pay tonight," He yelled back at Mrs. Kithara.

Mrs. Kithara gave her husband a flabbergasted look and ran back upstairs. Mr. Kithara swung his sword as he walked back and forth in front of the woman. She held her breath, closing her eyes, preparing for the worst when Mr. Kithara lifted up his sword, yelled a Chinese expletive, and then it hit her face. It was cold, slimy, and wet and it hit her with a smack and slid down her face to the floor. She looked down at the floor and saw the tomato. She stared at it with awe. Then another tomato hit her forehead as she was looking down. She couldn't believe it. She was being attacked with killer vegetables by a wild Chinese man. She thought about that movie, "Attack of the Killer Tomatoes," but then he came toward her with celery stalks and started hitting her all over with them. She started to cry again. This was humiliating, plus she was hungry too. He turned his back to her. He was gathering something in his hand. His back was hunched over like Dr. Frankenstein's in the movies. He turned to her with two huge cucumbers. She let out a scream.

"Do you know what I'm gonna do with these?"

"No, please!" She begged and closed her eyes.

He turned from her again and lifted his sword. Soon he turned back to her and then it hit her. She felt the coolness of it touch her nose with a sting. It was a cucumber slice. He was throwing cucumber slices at her and they stung her face.

"STOP, PLEASE! THIS IS MADNESS!"

Then the police busted in and rounded her up along with Mr. and Mrs. Kithara. They put them in a wagon and they were all arrested and arraigned for court.

Judge Franco was a busy man who had a lot on his plate, but he loved this time of year with a passion. He was in a hurry to get home to some fine cooking from his wife and was irritated by the three arguing defendants who were in his court.

"She murdered my snowmen!" yelled an irate Mr. Kithara.

"He kidnapped and tortured me!" yelled the lady.

The judge rapped his gavel for order in the court. "Mr. Kithara, tell me exactly what happened."

"She murdered my three snowmen. First, Mr. Snowman number one, which was the 587-6 model."

"Impressive," said the judge.

"She murdered Mr. Snowman number two, which was the 761-3 model."

"You had the 761-3 model? Those are hard to come by. Where do you shop?"

"At the Home Depot over on Hudspeth and Eighth. Then she murdered Ed, snowman number three, which was a super 47-8."

"A super 47-8? Young lady, I am charging you with assault with a deadly weapon."

"I didn't kill snowmen I and II. I killed Ed and he was only a snowman."

"Yes, and they are jolly happy souls."

"But what about him kidnapping me and torturing me with vegetables?" She asked.

"Mr. Kithara, I charge you with vegetable assault and fine you two bottles of bleu cheese dressing."

The courtroom erupted in laughter.

"NOW GET OUT OF MY COURTROOM!" The judge bellowed.

***

I looked out my window and smiled. This last week, Mr. and Mrs. Kithara apologized to me and convinced the judge to drop the charges. I looked across the street and watched Ed II smiling brightly at me as Mr. Kithara sat in a chair in front of him dressed in Chinese warrior gear with a shotgun across his lap, asleep.

Christmas was next week and despite all the hoopla that had happened, I was ready for a little normalcy. I was ready for smiling faces, kisses on cheeks, and running children. I was even ready for eggnog and spice cake, but most of all I was ready for Mr. Kithara to finally take down that snowman. Fat mother-fucker!

The End

COME AWAY WITH ME

She watched him as he went into her building. After a few minutes, she could see the silhouette of them kissing. She started to cry and pounded the steering wheel with her hands. She started the ignition, but the car wouldn't start. She got out of the car in frustration and then lifted the hood. She shook the battery cables and checked the radiator, but the car still wouldn't start. She left the car and started to walk through the park on her way home.

The park was dark and silent. *Too silent,* she thought to herself. She continued walking along the path and thought about him cheating on her. She wanted to cry, but thought she heard something behind her. She started to walk faster and realized she definitely heard something from behind. It flew past her. She screamed and started to run. It flew closer to her and she stopped, took out her mace and held it close. Then there was dead silence. She walked, looking behind and ahead of her, and then he grabbed her. She screamed and struggled as he wrestled her to the ground. He got on top of her and pulled her hair back. Her neck was exposed and he bit into it and started sucking.

At first, the pain was excruciating, but then the blood started leaving her body. She could feel the warmth of the blood as some of it drained to the back of her neck. The pain became pleasurable as he continued draining the life from her body. She moved with pleasure underneath him as he pushed her legs apart. Then he stopped, let out a howl, and flew away.

She lay there feeling nauseated and slowly got up. She walked for several blocks, and even though she was disoriented, she headed straight to her apartment. She entered and collapsed in her chair. She could not remember if what had happened was real or not. She went to bed.

Kenneth Bayless arrived at Vanessa Wilson's apartment at 8 o'clock. He opened the door and went in expecting to see her getting ready for work, but what he saw was a sickly looking woman in a wardrobe.

"What's wrong with you?" he asked.

"You cheated on me, you bastard! I saw you. I saw you at Stephanie's place. You get the hell out of here."

"It didn't mean anything, Vanessa."

"GET OUT! Give me my keys." She went toward him and collapsed in his arms.

"VANESSA, WHAT'S WRONG? WHAT'S WRONG?!" He shouted while holding her in his arms.

"I don't know. I feel so strange." She said and then passed out.

Kenneth lifted her up and rushed her to the hospital. He informed his job of the situation and waited for the doctors to tell them what was wrong with Vanessa. They came out an hour later and told him she needed a blood transfusion. They asked him if an animal of some sort had bitten her. He said he didn't know. He went to Vanessa's room and sat by her bed waiting until she regained consciousness.

"Where am I?" Vanessa said groggily as she stirred in her bed.

"You're in a hospital. Did an animal bite you? There're marks on your neck."

"I don't know. You were with Stephanie." She said starting to cry.

"I was stupid, Vanessa. Please forgive me. Please. I can't lose you." He said while kissing her face. She was too weak to resist and let him kiss and hold her until she fell asleep again.

***

Stephanie Baxter was on cloud nine. She had broken Kenneth and Vanessa up and now Kenneth was hers. He was an awesome lover and she wanted him forever. Stephanie hated Vanessa. She thought Vanessa was too goody-two-shoes. Everyone liked Vanessa, whereas she had to pick and choose her friends carefully because of her looks. *Gorgeous, I am,* Stephanie thought to herself and felt she could get any man she wanted and usually did, but Kenneth was different, he was kind and generous. A total Babe! It took some work. A lot of work, but she finally got under his skin. *Patience is the key,* she laughed to herself, *simply patience.*

While standing at the vending machine, two of her girlfriends came up. She couldn't wait to tell them. "Kenneth is mine." She said eagerly.

"Kenneth's at the hospital with Vanessa. She collapsed." One of her friends told her.

"What?"

"He's at the hospital with Vanessa." The other friend said exasperatedly.

"That can't be right. He must feel sorry for her." Stephanie said.

"Whatever." Her friends moaned in unison. "We're going back to work."

They walked off and Stephanie was left with a fury she had never felt before. She wanted to kill Vanessa. *She faked her illness on purpose,* she thought to herself. How could Kenneth do this to her? They were in love. How could he help that bitch? She would get even with Vanessa no matter what it took. She looked down at the sink across from the vending machine and saw a sharp knife. She took the knife and looked around. There was no one. She took the knife and sliced at her arm. *Just a little cut,* she thought to herself. The sting of the wound made her breathe deeply and the flow of blood relaxed her. "I'll get you, Vanessa. I'll get you."

***

Kenneth brought Vanessa home from the hospital and opened the door to her apartment. Vanessa was still a little reserved with him, but Kenneth made some tea for her, put her to bed, and slept on the couch while she slept quietly in the bedroom. Vanessa dreamed of oceans, of traveling through the sky and seeing mountains all over the world, and then she saw him and he called to her. "Vanessa," he called, "Vanessa." She woke up screaming. Kenneth rushed into the room.

"Baby, what's wrong?"

"HE'S HERE! HE'S HERE!"

Kenneth looked around the room quickly, but no one was there.

"I don't see anyone, Vanessa."

She started to cry. She remembered little things about the park and told him about it. Kenneth took her back to the hospital and had her examined as a possible rape case, but they found nothing except the unusual marks on her neck. The police were called and they made a report, but they told the doctors the evidence was sketchy. Kenneth took Vanessa home and held her in his arms while she cried.

"I'm changing, Kenneth. I can feel it," she said to him.

"They found nothing wrong with your blood. You've just been through a lot.

Give it time."

"I'm so frightened. I feel like I'm on fire. I think I can hear the heartbeats of birds as they fly by. He's after me, Kenneth. Don't let him take me, please. I love you. I love you so much." She said holding him tighter.

"I won't let anything happen to you."

"Promise?"

"I promise, darling. Hush now. Try to rest," he said while caressing her in his arms.

A couple of days had passed and Vanessa was feeling better. Kenneth's friend from college was coming into town and they were going out to party at a new club, called Rising. His name was Vilad and he was an odd sort. At first, he was very warm toward Vanessa, but then he saw the marks on her neck and stepped back two paces. Kenneth asked what was wrong and he simply said it was nothing then smiled and offered gifts to both of them.

They all seemed to be in a jolly mood as they entered the club. Kenneth and Vanessa both noticed how Vilad reacted to her neck wounds, but pretended it didn't happen. They ordered drinks at the bar and talked. Kenneth and Vilad went to the restroom and left Vanessa sitting at the bar. A very handsome man walked up to her and asked her to dance. At first she said no, but there was something familiar about him that she couldn't resist. She followed him to the dance floor. A hypnotic song with an unusual sound started playing and they danced. He held her close and they gyrated to the rhythm of the music. He pulled her closer; she closed her eyes and felt like she was soaring through skies across oceans and over mountains. He whispered, "Vanessa, you're mine." She pulled away from him immediately, looked at him, and ran.

"IT'S HIM! IT'S HIM! HELP!" Vanessa screamed as Kenneth and Vilad ran to her.

"Where is he?" Kenneth said.

"On the dance floor."

"Where, Vanessa?" Kenneth asked.

Vanessa looked around the dance floor and the man wasn't there. "He was right there," she said.

They called the police and they took a report and told Vanessa to come to the police station so that an artist could draw a likeness of him. Afterward, Kenneth and Vilad took Vanessa home. Vanessa sat with her head in her hands.

"He said 'you're mine'. He's coming after me."

"I must tell you something, my friend. She has been bitten." Vilad said grimly.

"Bitten by what?" asked Kenneth.

"She wears the mark of a vampire."

"Vampires? They're not real."

"They are, my friend. I have fought them on many continents and he is after Vanessa. She is not safe. He will attack her again, and soon. We must not leave her alone."

"Vampires are not real," Kenneth said.

"My friend, do not doubt me. Vanessa's life is in danger. I will go and get the needed items to protect her."

Vilad left to retrieve the items while Kenneth watched Vanessa and saw the expression of concern on her face.

"You can't believe what he's talking about?" Kenneth said.

"I do believe. I'm changing. I can feel it day by day. He's coming to get me."

"No one is going to take you away from me, Vanessa."

"Why shouldn't I let him take me? You didn't think of me when you were with Stephanie. Would you even be here if you hadn't found me sick the other morning?"

"Yes, I would be here. I love you."

"Then why did you cheat on me, Kenneth?"

"I thought I wanted her. I took for granted how much you meant to me."

"You know this all started the night you went to her place and I followed you there. Now this thing is after me."

"I know this is my fault. I did something stupid and now I may lose the love of my life. Don't let him take you. Please darling, don't let him take you." Kenneth said while going to Vanessa to hold her in his arms.

He held her close and whispered a silent prayer. Vilad came in with a big bag of crucifixes, garlic, and other mystical items for protection. They put garlic and crucifixes all over Vanessa's room. Vilad made a candlelit altar and said an ancient chant of protection for her. They put Vanessa to bed and left her bedroom door open while they waited in the living room. The night crept by very slowly. Vilad fell in and out of sleep on the couch while he handled with a wooden stake. Kenneth sat quietly fixated on Vanessa's room, and then he heard it faintly, a primeval tune that stirred his soul. Vilad instantly fell unconscious. Kenneth tried to fight it by rushing to Vanessa's room, but then he fell unconscious before reaching her door.

Vanessa stirred in her sleep and awakened to find the vampire outside her window. She tried to scream, but nothing would come out. He was singing a hypnotic tune to her with his eyes. She suddenly had no will of her own and removed the crucifixes and garlic from her bedside. She went to the window, opened it, and he floated in slowly and grabbed her in his arms. He laid her in the bed, got on top of her, and started caressing her breast and neck. He entered her and she moaned with pleasure. He thrust deeper inside of her and she was taken to worlds known and unknown. He arched her back to expose her neck and bit down on it hard. The pain turned to pleasure quickly and Vanessa welcomed him even deeper. Blood ran down her shoulders and stained her white satin sheets. She wrapped her legs around him and bent her neck even further. It was divine dying.

Kenneth awoke, rushed to Vanessa's room, and started screaming her name. There was a pool of blood dripping from below her neck down to the floor. She was barely breathing. Kenneth gathered her up in his arms and rocked her. Vilad rushed into the room and saw Vanessa's condition.

"My friend, it is too late. She will become a creature of the night by nightfall."

"NO! I WON'T LET HIM TAKE HER!"

"There is only one thing we can do. We must find this creature and destroy it."

"Where can we find him? He could be hiding in a million places."

"Stay here with Vanessa. I will contact an old friend."

As Vilad left, Kenneth washed Vanessa and changed her sheets. She lay in and out of conscious all day just mumbling and groaning. In another voice, she yelled "SHE IS MINE!" and started laughing. Kenneth sat beside her and a deep sadness of loss came upon him. *This is too great a price to pay for his error,* he thought to himself. He thought about Stephanie. She smiled at him, made him feel good, and fed his ego, but she could be any person in a million. Vanessa was his life. They shared an intimacy that kept them bonded from day to day. He now wished he had made her his wife and built a lifetime of love with her. Life could be so unforgiving at times. It did what it wanted to, when it wanted to, and how it wanted to, and you had no choice in the matter. If you were lucky, you grabbed and took what you wanted while you could, because life had a way of snatching whatever plans or thoughts away from you in the matter of a human mistake.

***

Vilad was at the deepest and darkest part of the city where the shadows had shadows. He was searching for someone, an old friend or enemy, one of them. He had come across so many of them, the vampires. *I'm so tired,* he thought to himself. He wanted a life, but she was his life and they killed her for revenge. They took his life away when they took her, and he had vowed to fight them until his dying day.

Mortis was different. He was a vampire with a soul. He had been a priest in Africa working with the poor before they turned him. When his people got to him, they were going to burn him alive, but Vilad rescued him and now he owed him. He didn't know if he was the same. The hunger had a way of turning even the righteous into monsters.

Vilad climbed down a long stairway to a dark and sinister looking door. It opened before he could knock and a small, troll-like woman beckoned for him to enter. She pointed the way to Mortis. Mortis welcomed him with fangs bared. He had completely turned.

"Vilad, my friend, are you protected?" He asked and Vilad nodded. "Of course you are protected. What can I do for you, my friend?"

Vilad held up the police drawing of the vampire.

"That is Gothas, a nasty sort. You must be careful, my friend. I would hate to see you lose your life."

"Where can I find him?"

"He is in the caves of Ester. He will be well protected."

"Have you succumbed to the hunger, my friend?" Vilad asked.

Mortis turns back into the innocent priest he first met in Africa. "I try to fight the hunger, Vilad. I try to fight it." Mortis says then transforms back into a vampire. "You have killed many of us. We are even, my friend. Go, to the hunt and the hunted."

"To the hunt and the hunted, my friend. Goodbye."

Vilad returned to Vanessa's apartment to find her tied up with ropes and lying on the floor. Kenneth was there with a frantic look on his face.

"She tried to attack me," Kenneth said.

"Here, my friend. We must enclose her in the pentagon and circle of protection," Vilad said while taking out some red sand and then drawing a circle and a pentagon within it. "Put her in the middle of it."

Kenneth lifted Vanessa's semi-conscious body and put her in the middle of the circle while Vilad said an ancient chant. Vanessa moaned in agony until she lost consciousness.

"Come, while she is unconscious, step into the hallway," Vilad advised.

As they entered the hallway outside Vanessa's apartment, they did not notice Stephanie listening around the corner.

"I know where to find this vampire. He is in the caves of Ester. We must kill him while it is still light outside. It will be dangerous though," Vilad said.

"I'm willing to go, but what about Vanessa? We cannot leave her here. She is unprotected."

"As long as she is in the circle, she will not turn into a vampire. She will be safe. Besides, it is still light outside. We must hurry."

Kenneth looked in on Vanessa and saw that she was still unconscious. He locked the door and left with Vilad. Stephanie came around the corner and slowly approached Vanessa's door and unlocked it. She stepped into the apartment cautiously and closed the door behind her. She watched Vanessa in the circle of protection and curiosity made her step closer. She noticed the circle was made of some sort of red sand. She scraped a little of the sand with her feet. "Not yet," she told herself aloud. "Not yet." She walked around the circle slowly and spoke.

"Little Miss Vanessa turning into a vampire. In case you're wondering how I got in, I made a copy of your boyfriend's keys that night he made love to me all night long. I figured I just might need them—and I was right. There you lay and here I stand. If you had not gotten sick, he would be with me now. He only feels sorry for you. He truly loves me. We are soul mates. You will never have Kenneth. I will see to it, Miss Perfection."

Stephanie looked around the apartment, gathered what she needed, and sat and waited.

***

They approached the cave slowly. They could smell rot and decay as they entered. Something was coming their way. Someone or something was walking as if they were dragging something. Kenneth and Vilad hid behind a boulder as the person walked by. The person was huge with a monstrous head and he drug a sack that carried something large. They hid until it passed by. They moved deeper into the cave until they heard a growl behind them. The growl seemed to be getting closer and closer. Vilad yelled, "RUN!" They ran for their lives.

***

Vanessa stirred awake. Her ropes had been removed. She tried to move beyond the circle, but could not. She looked up in surprise and saw Stephanie standing beyond the circle.

"Hello, Vanessa. How are you doing? Heard you've been bitten by a vampire? That must be awfully painful," Stephanie said while Vanessa groaned. "Tell me, do you hunger for blood? Does it drive you insane for the taste? Well, let's just see how much." She took a sharp knife and cut her wrist. Blood started seeping down to the floor. Vanessa looked at the blood and then looked away, but then stared back again mesmerized by the flow. Each drip to the floor made a loud bang to her ears. "STOP!" she screamed and grabbed her ears.

Stephanie laughed and said, "Here. Let me cut the other one," and sliced the other wrist with a knife. "Oh, that feels so good. The blood relaxes me so much. What does it do for you?"

Vanessa started breathing heavily and her hands started growing long nails. Her hair grew longer and her teeth were turning into fangs. When she had turned completely, she stood up and faced Stephanie.

"There, that's how you do it," Stephanie said and stabbed herself twice on the side of her neck. As blood seeped slowly from the wounds, Vanessa moved toward her, but stopped because she was confined to the circle of protection.

"What a neat little circle. Made of some sort of red sand and all I have to do is wipe it away. Hmmm, Kenneth will never be yours." She scraped the red sand away with her foot. Vanessa stepped forward and bit her on the neck.

***

Kenneth and Vilad were running from the growling noise and going deeper into the cave when they came upon a door. They entered it quickly and shut the door behind them. A coffin was inside. Vilad went to the coffin and removed the top while Kenneth stood at the door.

"It's him," Vilad said as the growling came closer.

"You have to hurry!" Kenneth cried.

Whatever was growling had come to the door and started pushing against it.

"HURRY!"

Vilad retrieved his wooden stake and hammer and placed it over Gothas' heart, but Gothas opened his eyes and started fighting Vilad. Whatever was outside of the door was pushing harder to get in while Kenneth was using all his strength to hold the door closed.

"HURRY, VILAD!"

Vilad gathered his strength and hammered at Gothas' chest. Gothas screamed and grabbed at the stake but Vilad struck again and again. The growling subsided as Gothas lay dying. Vilad retrieved his sword and cut off the vampire's head. They hurried back to Vanessa.

When they returned to the apartment, they noticed the door was unlocked. They entered and found Stephanie dead and Vanessa feeding off of her.

"She had the blood!" Vanessa cried.

Vilad started coming toward her to destroy her, but Kenneth stopped him.

"NO! NO! Please, man, I love her. Please. Have you never loved? Please, Vilad. Please," Kenneth begged while Vilad watched Vanessa.

He then looked at the desperate Kenneth and said, "For now, my friend. Just for now. Goodbye." Vilad left and decided he wanted to go back to the caves of Ester and see what that giant had been dragging in his bag.

Kenneth looked at Vanessa and shed a tear. He managed to get Vanessa and Stephanie in his car and drove to a nearby forest. He chopped off Stephanie's head and buried her. He drove far away and then stopped and let Vanessa out of his car. He stood beside her and held her.

"You can't go with me. You can't be a part of my world," Vanessa said through fanged teeth.

"This is my fault. What did I do to us?"

"I have to go, Kenneth."

"No! Don't leave me. You're my life."

"Goodbye," she said and flew away.

Kenneth chased after her saying, "Come back. Please, come back. I love you. I love you."

He stood crying in the night and Vanessa flew behind him. He turned around and she bit him. He turned a day later and Vanessa was there to greet and smile at him. They went out into the darkness and spread their wings. Someone was playing Norah Jones' "Come Away with Me" on a car radio and they did a dance of birds in the night sky playing as the tune carried them higher and higher. And Norah sang:

Come away with me in the night
Come away with me
And I will write you a song

Come away with me on a bus
Come away where they can't tempt us
With their lies

I want to walk with you
On a cloudy day
In fields where the yellow grass grows knee-high
So won't you try to come

Come away with me and we'll kiss
On a mountaintop
Come away with me
And I'll never stop loving you

And I want to wake up with the rain
Falling on a tin roof
While I'm safe there in your arms
So all I ask is for you
To come away with me in the night
Come away with me

And they flew into the night in each other's arms toward forever.

The End

VAMPIRE LOVE

Belinda Lewis had seen it all at her little wedding chapel outside of Las Vegas. Two gay Elvi, a Cher and a Liberace, a Madonna and a Cyndi Lauper, every mix of couple you can conceive of, she had seen and married them. Tonight was a quiet night, or so she had hoped. She stood at the lectern and played with the little cross her niece had made for her. It was made of two Popsicle sticks and colorful yarn. Her niece had told her it was for protection.

She stood with her head down looking at the colorful crucifix and did not notice the woman who had come into the chapel.

"Oh, you startled me."

"I'm sorry. Could you remove that object? It's shining in my eyes." The woman pointed at the cross on the table.

"Sure I can." Belinda said and removed the cross and put it behind the choir stand.

"I'm waiting on someone. He is always late."

Belinda noticed the woman was very beautiful, but awfully pale.

"Been vacationing in Alaska lately? Don't have much of a tan."

"No. I haven't been to Alaska in centu-, I mean years." She said and just then a man came running into the chapel out of breath.

"I'm sorry I'm late." The man said breathless.

"You are always late."

"Are you ready?" he asked.

"I don't know," she said and sat down on the pew sulking.

"Ah, come on, Mo. We agreed."

"I wanted to get married two centuries ago. Now I don't know."

Belinda looked at the woman as if she was insane. *Two centuries ago. What the heck is she talking about? Boy, he's about as pale as her.* She thought to herself. She looked at them and giggled on the inside. She had seen one member of the couple always stall so many times, but in the end they always gave in.

"Now, now people. Let's take a couple of deep breaths and relax. Everything's going to be fine," Belinda said.

"Come on, Mo," the man begged.

"You bit that blonde in Nova Scotia."

"Oh, no! Not the blonde in Nova Scotia!"

"I told you not to bite her."

"That was two hundred years ago and you're still complaining about the blonde in Nova Scotia. Was it even Nova Scotia back then?"

"You bite anything that comes your way."

"If someone offers me free neck, why shouldn't I take free neck?"

"You're a wolf."

"I'm a vampire for corn's sake. That's what we do." He stopped and stared at Belinda who stood there in shock.

"You two are vampires?" She asked.

"Yes. Will you still marry us?" he asked.

She looked at them in awe for a couple of seconds then smiled. "Heck, if I can marry a Siegfried and a Diana Ross, I can surely marry two vampires."

"Who said I'd marry you?" The woman said.

"Ah, Mo, for Pete's sake." The man said exasperated.

"I told you not to bite her."

"Did I not chop off her head? I chopped off her head." The man said angrily.

Belinda looked at them dumbfounded and then beckoned the man to come to her.

"Hey, look, just apologize to her." Belinda advised.

"I've apologized for two hundred years."

"Trust me. Apologize and make it come from the heart."

The man went to his intended and knelt down in front of her.

"I apologize for the blonde in Nova Scotia. I didn't know it would hurt you that much. You're the only woman for me, Mo. I love you and I want to spend forever with you. Again. You are my soul mate. Will you marry me?"

She looked at him, smiled, and said, "Yes."

The man picked the woman up and swung her around in elation.

"Ugh, how long you two been together?" Belinda asked.

"843 years." The woman proudly proclaimed.

"Damn, that's a lot of milk. Anyway, you two stand right here." Belinda said as they stood in front of the lectern. "Do you take uh-"

"Morticia Valinsky."

"To be your wedded wife?"

"I do."

"And do you take uh-"

"Boris Doranis."

"To be your wedded husband?"

"I do."

"Well, I now pronounce you man and uh. Man and uh-. I pronounce you thing and thing. You're married."

"Oh my, we're married!" The woman said.

"Kiss her. Kiss her." Belinda said and they kissed passionately.

They all started laughing.

"Boy, I'm hungry." The woman said and they both stared at Belinda.

Belinda yelled "Aaah!" and ran to the side of the pew clutching her niece's cross.

They both laughed and flew out the chapel by crashing through the roof. Belinda looked at the hole in her roof and shook her head.

"All kinds. I've married all kinds. Now how am I going to explain that to the insurance company?"

The End

I HAVE SEEN THE MOUNTAINTOP

This flight was tedious. The food on my tray bounced from one hole to the next and my green Jell-O had mixed with the turkey and gravy, making it look like a gangrene Thanksgiving. I had ridden many flights and experienced many flight patterns, but this was one of the worst flights ever. I wanted to go home. That's all I wanted, just to experience my little cubbyhole of an apartment and rub my pet cat, Sam, one more time. I hoped Mrs. Cole was still feeding her. She promised she would do so during her daily bridge game. I honestly believe her group of elderly friends were secret professional gamblers judging by the way they habitually and punctually attended her bridge games. I thought about Carol briefly. Would I call her when I got back home? I didn't know. We were in between making this relationship permanent or letting go. I didn't know what I wanted to do. We had fun together and that was the problem. Did we have what it took to make it a permanent thing?

The plane bumped and grinded it's way to Philadelphia. My turkey and gravy had completely turned into the Incredible Hulk when the "Fasten Your Seat Belt" light came on again. The stewardess quickly took away the passengers' trays. I wasn't worried. I had flown too many times and saw too many "Fasten Your Seat Belt" signs. The plane took a violent jolt to the left and everyone screamed and got even louder. The stewardesses were trying to keep everyone calm by assuring them that everything was alright when the plane took another jolt to the left, and this one was more violent than the first. This time even I became alarmed, and then the pilot came on the intercom in a calm voice and said everything was fine. He was still explaining that we were just experiencing some technical difficulty when the plane took another violent jolt to the left and went rushing down toward the mountains up ahead.

I don't know what went through my mind as we were hurled downward. I think I prayed aloud. I think I screamed. I think I cried. I woke up to a severely cold wind. I was still strapped to my seat. Half of the plane was gone and there were people missing from seats that had been ripped out. I looked to my right and the guy next to me was dead, his broken neck bent forward at an odd angle. I quickly unbuckled myself and started yelling for help. There was no one, just the bitter cold and snow on top of a mountain. I looked to the back of the plane and there were dead bodies strapped to chairs. Their necks had also been broken or they had been hit by pieces of airplane. I was alone in a freezer graveyard.

I was lucky. The sun was coming up. Surely there were rescue efforts on the way. I walked around my iceberg desert and saw more mountains and snow. That's it, just mountains and snow. I was going to freeze to death by nightfall if the rescue team did not arrive. I walked back into the broken airplane and looked around for something to make a fire. The dead stared at me with horror-ridden eyes. I had to do something. I started closing the eyes of the dead and covering their bodies with blankets I found on the plane, but I ran out of blankets and couldn't cover them all. There was a space in the back of the plane that felt warmer than the rest so I stayed there most of the day. When I became hungry, I searched purses, bags, and overhead compartments for food. I found mints, candy, crackers, beef jerky, and a ham sandwich that I was reluctant to eat but I eventually let it find its way to my stomach. I tried to save some of my food stash because I didn't know how long I would be on top of this mountain.

I found many cell phones, but got no signal at this altitude. I tried to stay awake as much as I could, but the cold made me sleepy all the time. I took blankets off the dead and made a nice pallet in the back of the plane. I just wanted to sleep for a little while. All those blankets kept me somewhat warm, but I knew the cold night air would be a problem. I didn't care. I just wanted to sleep for a very long time.

I awakened to a noise in the dark. It was a snatching sound up from the head of the plane. I went to investigate. Luckily the moon was shining and I had some light. I looked out from the edge of the plane and nothing was out of the ordinary except for the bitter cold that I felt to my bone. I turned to walk back to the rear of the plane and noticed that the dead man who had been sitting next to me on the plane was missing. I stood there in shock because I knew he was dead. He could not have gotten up and walked away from the plane. He was dead.

I started looking around the plane for a flashlight so I could search for the man. He must have been in a coma or something, woke up in shock, and was now wandering around in the snow. I searched for a light in the backpacks, suitcases, and purses until I came across a mini-flashlight in a backpack. It still worked and shone a broad beam across the snow. I started searching and yelled for the man. There was nothing except for the eerie swirls of fog that danced across the snow and the mountains. I tried to look everywhere but the snow was soaking my pants and I was starting to feel tingling in my toes. I went back to the plane in hopes of changing into some more clothes when I noticed another body was missing. I stopped dead in my tracks and noticed the silence that strangled the night air. It was too quiet. Two bodies could not have come back from a coma. I stood and listened as the wind rustled across rocks and snow. I could just make out a faint sound, it sounded like something was chewing.

I rushed to the back of the plane. There was an animal out there and it was eating the dead bodies. I hid underneath the blankets until I heard a moaning noise and then someone started screaming. There was actually someone who had regained consciousness and he was screaming that he couldn't feel his legs. I was terrified to leave the blankets, but I had to quiet the man. He was drawing attention to the animal or animals.

I got out from under the blankets and rushed to the man. He was still saying he couldn't feel his legs. I hurriedly told him to be quiet because there was an animal out there that was eating the dead bodies. He then laughed and said, "There goes our meat supply!" I was taken aback for a second, and then I looked at the man and started unbuckling his seat belt. He asked me what I was doing. I told him I had to move him to the rear of the plane or the animals would get him. I started dragging the man and he only laughed and said, "They don't want me, I've got bony legs." I nearly dropped him at that statement. What kind of a character was this man that he could laugh at such adversity? I was terrified. This animal (or animals) wasn't eating the bodies at their seats. They were taking the bodies with them and eating them. I thought *what strength these animals must have!*

I put the man up against the wall and covered him and myself with blankets. He started laughing again and asked, "When the animals get through with the dead bodies, what are they going to eat on next?" For some reason, I started laughing myself. If the rescue effort wasn't here soon, we were going to become mush meat. We sat quietly for some time, just listening intently until we both fell asleep.

I don't know how long we were asleep, but I heard a slight rustling. I woke up the man next to me and told him to be quiet. A thick mist came into the plane and crawled over the seats. It came to a body and snatched it, suspending the body in midair then snatching it completely away. The man next to me screamed "What the fuck!" I told him to be quiet immediately because the thick mist was coming back. Then another body was snatched from its seat. Then we heard it, a slight stirring, a slight grunt, then chewing and grinding. The man next to me started crying, "We got to get out of here, but I can't move my legs!" I told him to be quiet and that I was going to search for a weapon. He begged me not to leave him. I told him to sit quietly and that I'd be right back.

I started searching the floor area of the plane in hopes of finding a rescue kit, but there was none. I did, however, find a big heavy flashlight when the mist started coming back. The man yelled for me to hurry back. I rushed to the rear of the plane and watched the mist from under the covers. Again, it snatched a body into midair and then snatched it forward. This went on all night long and the chewing and grinding was driving us insane.

There were only two bodies left. I managed to find an iron rod and kept it close by. I gave the man the flashlight to hold. The mist was back and the last two bodies were snatched away. The man next to me mumbled a loud "Ah shit." He asked me, "What are we gonna do?" I didn't have an answer. I just held the rod tightly in my hands. We heard the chewing again and then it stopped. There was complete silence for a long time. The guy next to me asked if I thought it was through eating. I didn't know. I just sat there terrified. How was I going to defend us against this beast?

For a brief second, I thought about luck. I thought about how we survived an airplane crash only to be eaten by a mystical beast. God had a sense of humor after all. I wanted to see my family again. I wanted to see my cat and, lastly, I wanted to see Carol. I needed her laughter and I needed her smile. I wanted to be in her arms again and to make love to her. Yes, life was serious and bad things happened and you needed someone to go through the bad times with you, but you also needed laughter. Laughter was a cure for all ailments and heartbreaks, and right now I needed to see her sweet face and hear her uninhibited laughter one more time.

Dawn was approaching. If we could make it to daylight, maybe the rescuers would be here. I thought too soon. The mist was coming back. The man next to me started screaming and I put a death grip on my piece of rod, then we saw it. It was 10 feet tall, solid white, with sharp fangs and claws. It grabbed the man by his legs. He screamed in terror as the monster lifted him and pulled him forward. I grabbed the man and pulled him back with all my strength. I couldn't pull the man and fight the monster at the same time, so I yelled to the man to hit the beast with the flashlight. He flailed wildly at the beast until the flashlight came on and shone in the beast's face. The beast let out a howl as the light hit its eyes and then it dropped the man to the ground. I said to the man, "It's the light! It's the light, and it's hurting his eyes." The man immediately started shining the light at the beast and the beast howled and ran away along with the mist.

We both lay there breathing hard. The man started laughing and said, "I hope these batteries are Duracell." I laughed a little too then grabbed the man and pulled him close to me. "Not bad," I told him. He said, "Thanks."

We could finally see the dawn. It was a beautiful display of God's mercy. We both lay there breathing heavily until we heard a humming sound. The humming sound was getting closer. It was the most beautiful sound in the world. It was a rescue helicopter. I got up and ran to the front of the plane and waved my blanket back and forth. They flashed a light my way. I started laughing with joy.

My companion turned out to be a famous comedian and he promised me a boatload of treasures. They examined me and found I had a slight frostbite on my toes. I was lucky. They were not going to remove them. We were accosted by the press but they were mostly interested in the comedian. After all the hoopla, I returned home to hugging and crying family members. Carol was there and she ran into my arms. I held her for what seemed like an eternity. We all celebrated until the midnight hour and then everyone went home. Carol and I were left alone. We made love until the morning hour. She then cried in my arms and told me she'd become whatever I wanted her to become. I told her to be herself and savor life the way she always does and that I'd love her sweet smile forever.

Yes, I have seen my mountaintop and it was filled with an awareness of life that I had never known. I can laugh in tribulation and smile in heartbreak now. I am a survivor and I can only find joy in that.

The End

ABOUT THE AUTHOR

D. Wilburn was born in Dallas, TX. She attended and graduated from Paul Quinn College with a B.S. Degree in Secondary Education with minors in English and Math. She has taught school for five years. She is a single parent of one child. She has written poetry, songs, and numerous screenplays.